FINDING LOVE WITH THE BILLIONAIRE

A CLEAN BILLIONAIRE ROMANCE

ANNE-MARIE MEYER

To My Writing Buddies
Without you, I'd be a crazy and lonely writer

GRAB A FREE NOVELLA BY ANNE-MARIE MEYER

Sign up for Anne-Marie Meyer's newsletter and receive her novella, Love Under Contract (A Swan Princess Inspired Novella), FREE!

Take me to my FREE novella

GRAB ALL 5 SWEET BILLIONAIRE ROMANCES FOR $9.99

If you love swoon worthy, clean romance, grab all 5 Sweet Billionaire Romances for only $9.99! Free in KU.

That's a $5.00 savings!

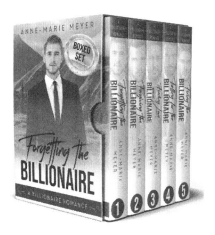

Head over to Amazon HERE

CHAPTER ONE

MADELINE

*M*adeline stood inside of the elevator, tapping her toes along with the music. She shifted her weight and brought her thumbnail up to chew on it. Why had Parker asked her in on a Saturday? Lead editors never did that. And if they did, it was for a good reason. As much as she tried to squelch her excitement, the words *huge, career-changing story* kept rolling around in her mind.

Maybe Bridget, her roommate, had been right. There was no need to work herself up if it was nothing. She took a deep breath and dropped her hand to smooth down her skirt. There had to be a problem with her recent article. That was all.

But Parker wanted to talk to her in person—on a Saturday. *Career-changing story* made its way back into her mind.

Before she slipped into madness from trying to dissect his intentions, the elevator dinged and the doors opened. She stepped into the foyer of *The Journal*, one of Seattle's well-known magazine headquarters.

The front lobby was eerily quiet today. Lola, the front receptionist, wasn't sitting at her desk where the phones usually were ringing off the hook every ten seconds. The water cooler was full, and no fellow journalists were standing around it, trying to look as if they weren't procrastinating their latest story.

Even the dog was curled up in the corner.

Madeline stopped as her heart picked up speed. Wait. Dog? She eyed the fluffy black-and-brown animal that was sprawled across the floor. It was massive, burying half of the entryway mat under its body. Its mouth was open, allowing its tongue to drape across the marble floor. Its chest rose and fell.

Her throat constricted. Why was there a dog in the building? Glancing around, she saw no owner. Fear raced up her spine as she slipped over to the door, praying that the animal won't wake up.

One in every seventy-five people gets bitten by a dog.

She allowed that thought to linger for a moment before she pushed it out. Reciting facts had been a coping method she'd started to use as a child to deal with situations the made her uncomfortable. Now, as a twenty-six-year-old, it was just annoying. But her brain didn't seem to realize that.

She grasped the metal handle and pulled. The sound of voices carried down the hall. Slipping into the hallway, she made her way toward the open door—Parker's office.

"I'm really excited that we could come to an arrangement, Mr. Davenport," Parker said with a hint of desperation in his normally icy tone.

Madeline paused. *Davenport.* Where had she heard that name recently?

"I'm ready to put this whole situation in the past," a deep, smooth voice responded.

Madeline took a breath as she waited just outside Parker's open door. Whatever he wanted her to do, she would take the assignment gracefully. After all, her time doing grunt work had to come to an end at some point. Right?

She stepped in front of the open door and located Parker. He had his chair pulled up to his desk and was resting his elbow in front of him. His smile was huge. She couldn't help but stare at him.

Since when did he smile?

Two people sat in front of him with their backs to her. One had dark hair that was tousled in a purposeful way. His shoulders were tight under his suit coat, and every so often he'd turn his attention to the massive picture windows to the right.

The woman next to him had bright white hair that flipped up at the end. Stress permeated off her perfect posture and meticulous movements.

"Madeline!" Parker said when his gaze landed on her in the doorway. He raised his arm and waved her in. "I'm glad you finally made it." He gave her a pointed look. It was similar to the one he would always give her when she turned her article in five minutes after the deadline.

She stepped into the room and both visitors turned. The mysterious man stood, and his gaze landed on her. Now she knew where she'd heard his name before. Liam Davenport, also known as the billionaire playboy forced to give up his wild ways to run his late father's outdoor supply company. He had been in the papers for weeks.

Unfortunately for Madeline, she was privy to all of his dirt. Bridget had been more than happy to read her every last salacious tidbit about him. Even down to whether he preferred boxers or briefs. Madeline's cheeks heated as she dropped her gaze away from his suit that seemed tailored to fit him perfectly.

Parker. Story. Get your head on straight, Madeline.

"Madeline Abernathy, this is Liam Davenport and his business associate Alice Pickering," Parker said.

She nodded but kept her back against the far wall. She wasn't sure why she was here, so she didn't want to intrude. What could she possibly offer Liam Davenport?

Liam stepped away from his chair. "Here. You can have my seat," he said as he pulled at his collar. His suit coat was unbuttoned, exposing creases in his white shirt. Madeline tried not to stare. She knew very little about billionaires, but she was sure they didn't wear wrinkly clothes.

She raised her hand. "Oh, no. That's okay. I'm fine here."

He gave her one of his million-dollar—or she should say billion-dollar—smiles. "I insist."

She glanced over to Parker who widened his eyes and tilted his head toward the seat.

"Thanks," she said as she slipped onto the chair.

Alice cleared her throat and turned back to Parker. She had on designer glasses, and her lips seemed perpetually pinched. "You were saying, Mr. Green."

Parker nodded. "Yes. This is Madeline Abernathy. She's one of the best journalists I've had in years."

Alice's pretentious gaze swept over Madeline and, for a moment, Madeline felt exposed. How did people do that? Steal all of a person's confidence with one look. She shifted in her seat as heat crept up her back.

"She's really the best? Because the *best* is the only thing that can get us out of this mess," Alice said as her gaze landed on Liam.

Madeline snuck another look at him. He had a pained expression as he stood in front of the window, staring out at the setting sun. The lights of Seattle shimmered against the darkening sky.

Parker slammed his hands down on the table, and Madeline jumped. "It's settled then. She'll leave first thing tomorrow morning."

Realizing that her life was being planned without her, Madeline straightened. "I'm sorry. What?"

Alice sighed again. Madeline felt her confidence wavering.

Parker smiled. "You will be covering a story for Mr. Davenport. They are headed to Alaska tomorrow morning, and you will be with them." He steadied his gaze on her.

Still not understanding, Madeline leaned forward. "Alaska? Why would we be going to Alaska?"

Alice leaned toward Parker. "Is she really the best journalist you have?"

"Alice, stop it," Liam said as he turned toward them. He had loosened his tie and left it to hang around his neck. The top button of his shirt had been undone, and he looked more relaxed. He extended his hand. "Ms. Abernathy, thanks for coming in."

Madeline eyed his hand. Then allowed her gaze to trail up his arm to his face. Somewhere, deep inside, she melted a bit. The tabloids didn't do him justice. He was handsome. In an unkempt, outdoorsy kind of way.

When she didn't respond, he shot her a half-smile, which caused her cheeks to burn. Embarrassed, Madeline shot out her hand and shook his, hoping he didn't notice what he had just done to her emotions.

"Nice to meet you, Mr. Davenport. I have to say, the newspapers are making a killing off your most recent stories," she said as she allowed herself to meet his gaze.

His shoulder's tightened, and he dropped her hand. An uncomfortable look flashed over his face. But just as quickly as it came, it disappeared. He leaned in. "Well, don't believe everything you read. You should know that by now."

"That's why they're here," Parker said, breaking the trance that Liam Davenport put on her. Madeline turned and focused her attention on what her editor was saying. "They need to do some . . . damage control," he continued.

"Against what?" Madeline asked, glancing around to Alice then Liam. What scandalous information could the press have about Liam that they hadn't already reported on?

Liam grew agitated and started pacing the room.

Alice cleared her throat. "There's information that is set to be released tomorrow. It's about some practices Liam's late father had gotten wrapped up in." She turned to stare at Madeline.

"Practices? Like, illegal things?" Madeline's voice trailed off as she studied Alice.

Alice's expression tightened as she nodded.

Glancing over at Liam, Madeline saw a flat look settle in his gaze. Her heartbeat slowed. She felt sorry for him. "What does it have to do with Alaska?"

Alice tapped her pen on the planner in front of her. "We will be holding a press conference in Denali tomorrow morning. You won't fault me if I don't give you specifics right now. In general terms, you will be coming to write the article about what you see. Paint Davenport Outdoors in a positive light. Hopefully, we can help combat the negative response that this information is sure to stir up."

Madeline cringed. A puff piece? That's what Parker had called her here to write? She eyed him, but the huge smile he had plastered on his lips didn't falter. He knew this was beneath her. Why did he suggest she write it? "You thought I'd be the best one to cover this?" she asked.

Parker narrowed his eyes at her and then the cheesy expression was back. "Yes. Of course you're the best for this story."

Madeline felt as if she were going to be sick. Is that all Parker saw her as? One of the girls that he'd hired to start writing that tasteless dribble the magazine had started printing? And here she thought she was making headway. She gritted her teeth. Why did she allow herself to hope that he'd give her a break? Oh, right. She deserved it.

A phone chimed next to her. Alice raised it to her cheek. "Hello?" she said as she stood. After a second, she covered her phone with her hand. "I should take this in the hall." Clutching her planner to her chest, she slipped out the door.

"I'm going to use the facilities," Liam said as he followed after her.

As soon as the room was empty, Madeline zeroed in on Parker. His gaze flitted from her face then toward the window.

"What? Just say it," he said, sighing.

"Seriously? I'm supposed to make billionaire bad boy look good?" She stood and started to pace. Her body was hot with anger.

"They're making a sizable donation to the magazine in exchange for this story. I'm bumping other articles so I can run it next week."

Madeline's muscles tensed. Did that mean he was bumping her story about the waste that was mysteriously getting dumped into the ocean? She narrowed her eyes. "Come on, Parker. We're not that kind of magazine. We print good stories. Not crap to help people cover up the horrible things they've done."

He avoided her gaze as he straightened a pile of papers on his desk. "It's what has to happen if we want to keep afloat so we can run the stories that actually matter."

Madeline chewed her nail. "But Liam Davenport is ridiculous. I saw the stories about him crashing his father's yacht when he was supposed to be attending his father's funeral. No amount of journalistic finesse can make that guy look good."

Parker's face paled as his gaze raced over to the door. "Mr. Davenport," he said through clenched teeth. "I hope you found that the restrooms were up to your standards."

Madeline felt light-headed as she turned around to see that Liam had returned. He had his arms folded across his chest, and he was leaning against the open door. Her heart pounded as he studied her.

He kept his gaze trained on her as he pushed off the doorframe and entered. "It was a little *ridiculous*, but I managed to figure out where it was." His voice was low as he shot her a pointed look.

"I'm—"

He raised his hand. "Listen, Ms. Abernathy. You don't have to like me. You don't even have to talk to me. But what's about to break tomorrow has nothing to do with me and will hurt a lot of people whose livelihood depends on Davenport Outdoors to stay afloat." He slipped off his suit coat and hung it over his arm. "So, do you think your journalistic finesse can bring itself down to our lowly level and save those jobs?"

Heat raced up her spine and into her cheeks. She pinched her lips shut and nodded. "I never intended—"

"On me hearing. Yeah, I figured that." He turned to Parker. "Thank you for being so accommodating. I look forward to putting this all behind us."

Parker stood and extended his hand. "As do I." They shook hands.

Liam turned and started for the door. Just when he was a few inches from Madeline, he stopped. His dark brown eyes met hers. For no logical reason, her knees weakened. Her mind screamed at her to run, but she stayed rooted in her spot.

"Ms. Abernathy, I will see you tomorrow at the airport at six a.m. sharp." He paused then made his way to the door.

She nodded. There was no way she was going to be able to muster any words out of her muddled brain.

Once he was gone, she turned to Parker, who smiled and said, "Well, this should be interesting."

CHAPTER TWO

LIAM

*A*lice was too busy speaking to the person on the other end of the call to talk to Liam, which he was grateful for. He walked behind her as they made their way down the hall and into the foyer. He tried not to get frustrated by her pace when all he wanted to do was get out of the building.

His suit was driving him crazy. He wanted to change into his normal clothes and get back to his normal life. He stifled a sigh as Alice pushed open the glass door. His normal life didn't exist anymore. Everything had changed.

It didn't help that Ms. Abernathy had gotten under his skin, and in more ways than one. Her bright green eyes and dusting of freckles seemed burned into his mind no matter how hard he tried to push them out.

Desperate for a distraction, he glanced around, located Duke, and whistled. This Bernese mountain dog was the one saving grace he had in his crazy life.

"Come, boy," he said, tapping his leg.

Duke whipped his head toward him and scrambled to get up.

The marble floor wasn't made for a dog and caused his feet to slip underneath him. When he finally righted himself, he bounded over to Liam who rubbed his head.

Alice gave him a pointed look as she tapped the down button for the elevator. She wasn't shy about showing her disdain for his insistence on bringing Duke where ever he went. Liam just smiled at her. She'd been with Davenport Outdoors since he was a boy. The PR executive and mother figure.

His birth mom died when he was three, and after his father divorced wife number five, Liam stopped counting on any woman to stay. Alice was the only constant person in his life. Well, after his father. But Richard Davenport was dead. Every newspaper seemed hell-bent on reminding him of that fact.

The elevator doors opened, and they stepped inside.

"Wait," Madeline's voice called out.

Liam shoved his hand in front of the doors. He hadn't even noticed she had entered the foyer. "Going down?" he asked, kicking himself for sounding so dumb.

She eyed Duke and then shook her head. "I'll get the next one."

Liam glanced around. "There's only one."

Her cheeks turned pink. "I meant, I'll catch this one . . . you know . . ."

"Just get on," Alice said as she tipped the phone from her lips.

Madeline stared at her and then over to Duke.

Liam curled his fingers around his dog's collar. "This help?" he asked. He knew Duke had no interest in Madeline. He was already half asleep as he sat next to Liam's leg.

The buzzing of the elevator filled the air.

"Come on, we won't bite," he said.

Madeline took one last cautious glance at Duke and then stepped on.

Liam dropped his arm and the elevator hummed to life. Madeline's face paled as the doors shut. She wrapped her arms around her chest and leaned into the corner.

"I'm losing you," Alice shouted. "Hello? Hello?" She groaned as she shoved her phone into her purse. "Well, that's just frustrating."

Liam glanced over at her. "Relax, Alice. You can't fix everything right now anyway."

She shot him a pointed look. "Liam Davenport, do you have any idea the nightmare that is about to come down on us?" She shook her head as she glanced over to Madeline and lowered her voice. "Your father left us a giant mess to clean up."

There was a tone to her voice that made him feel like he was in middle school again, getting scolded by his prep school teacher. He straightened. "I know."

She glanced over to him, and her expression softened. "Why would he do this to us? Why didn't he warn me? Now you're left picking up the pieces." She shook her head. "It's not right."

Liam moved his hand to rub Duke's head. His stomach was too knotted to say anything. When it came to his father, he preferred to not try to figure why he did what he did. It was always best to just walk away. Which was exactly what Liam had been doing until Alice called him three months ago to tell him that his dad had been in a car accident and didn't make it.

Suddenly, Liam went from having a carefree life, moving from country to country with no responsibilities and no one to disappoint, to being the CEO of a billion-dollar company. Who—as Alice would put it—was about to have the wrath of the ever-living world reign down on them.

Nothing like trial by fire.

"Did you know that escalators are more dangerous than elevators?"

Liam turned to Madeline who had her eyes pinched shut.

"What?"

"You're twenty times more likely to get injured on an escalator than in an elevator, which is silly because there are twenty times more elevators than escalators."

Liam glanced over to Alice who shrugged.

"Is that so, Ms. Abernathy?" Liam asked.

Madeline opened her eyes and nodded. Then she winced as if she had realized she'd spoken. "I'm sorry. I recite useless crap when I'm nervous."

A smile played on Liam's lips. She was nervous. Apparently, her stone-cold attitude toward him could be melted. This intrigued him.

Before he could prod further, the doors opened and Madeline bolted toward the door. Liam watched her retreating frame as she slipped out the front doors and disappeared into the crowd.

"Well, that was interesting," Alice said under her breath as she stepped off the elevator.

Liam whistled and waved to Duke as he followed after Alice. He found Ms. Abernathy intriguing, even if she'd just insulted him moments ago. They stepped out of the building and onto the side-walk where Daniel, his driver, was leaning against their limo, studying his phone.

"Daniel Douglas, get off that phone right now before I fire you," Alice said as she marched over to the limo door.

Daniel's face heated as he dropped his phone and glanced around. When his gaze fell on Liam, Liam shook his head and gave him a smile. Daniel looked relieved as he slipped his phone into his pocket and reached for the door.

"He's not going to save you," Alice said. Typical Alice. Even though she hadn't watched their interaction, she knew exactly what Liam was doing. She turned and gave him a pointed look before she slipped into the limo.

Liam gave Daniel another smile, which seemed to help bolster him up, and then he and Duke followed after Alice. Once they were situated, Daniel shut the door.

"He works for me," Liam said as he leaned back on the buttery leather seats.

Alice raised a brow.

Liam's resolve faltered. "Us. He works for us." Alice was the second largest shareholder.

She nodded. "Right."

Daniel pulled out onto the road, and they drove a few seconds before being forced to a stop. Horns honked as traffic piled in around them. Liam felt suffocated sitting in the limo in his suit. He tugged at his collar again, wishing he was climbing the mountains in Patagonia or surfing the waves in Australia.

"You're nervous," Alice said, nodding toward his fingers that were trying to free his neck from the confines of his shirt.

"What? Am not." He let his hand fall to the seat beside him. Alice's ability to pinpoint his emotions irritated him.

Trying to get ahold of himself, he sighed and glanced out the window. He needed to accept that his previous life was over. Living in an overpopulated city was now his future.

"Yes, you are," she said as she rifled through her bag and then triumphantly removed her chiming phone. After a few swipes, she lowered it. "I have some good news."

Liam glanced at her. "What?"

"Everything is set for tomorrow. We'll fly into Denali, you'll hold the press conference—I pray that Ms. Abernathy lives up to Mr. Green's confidence—and then we'll fly out. Hopefully, all this hard work will drown out the words *illegal poaching* and *endangered animals.*"

Liam straightened as her words raced through his mind. Leave it to his father to ruin the one thing Liam thought they'd shared together. Ever since he was seven years old, his dad had taken him hunting. He showed him how important it was to respect the animal. How to kill it and clean it. *You only kill an animal for food. Respect the animal, Liam.* The memory now left a sour feeling in his stomach. What a liar.

Well, how did you respect the endangered black rhino or South China tiger, Dad? He clenched his fists. If his dad were alive today . . .

Liam shook his head. If his dad were alive today, he'd just continue living his life, not caring about who he hurt.

Liam glanced over at Alice who was studying him. She sighed and took her glasses off. "He disappointed all of us," she said. Her voice was low. It was the first time in a long time that Liam saw some emotion in her expression.

He pushed his hand through his hair. "That was Dad." Liam forced a smile. "Let's talk about something else."

MADELINE

"Oh. My. Gosh," Bridget said as she stood in the middle of the kitchen in her bunny slippers and fluffy yellow robe.

Madeline dropped her purse on the table and walked past her. "Come on, Bri. It's not that big of a deal."

Bridget followed her into her room. "Not a big deal? Not a *big* deal?" She reached out and grabbed Madeline's arm. "You were in the same room as Liam Davenport." Her voice squeaked when she said his name.

Madeline stilled her nerves and turned. "Yes. I was in the same room as Liam Davenport." She paused as she let those words settle around her roommate. "And Parker and a woman named Alice." She gave Bridget an exasperated look as she pulled her arm from her and walked over to her closet. After searching around for a few seconds, she emerged with a suitcase.

Bridget sat on her bed with a dazed expression. "This is so surreal," she whispered.

"I think your crush is getting a bit out of hand," Madeline said as she dropped her suitcase on the bed and unzipped it.

"Out of hand?" Bridget gave her a shocked look. "Liam Davenport and I are destined to be together."

Madeline glanced over to her. "Destined?"

"Madame Tremone said she saw us together." Bridget clasped her hands in front of her. "Please introduce us."

Madeline stared at her. "Are you serious? You want me to introduce you to Liam Davenport because your psychic told you that you two were destined to be together?"

Bridget batted her eyelashes. "Please?"

Madeline shook her head. "I couldn't even if I wanted to. I'm meeting him at the airport tomorrow and then we're heading to Alaska."

Bridget dropped her hands on the bed. "Ugh. I should have been a reporter."

"Journalist," Madeline corrected.

Bridget gave her an exasperated look. "Journalist," she mocked.

Madeline nodded as she shoved some underwear into the suitcase. "I think you're a much better bartender."

"But all I get are drunk guys. You—you get billionaires."

Madeline's shoulders tightened. Going to Alaska to write a story to help soften the blow on a multibillion-dollar company wasn't exactly what she'd dreamed about in school. Writing the stories that changed minds and hearts—that had been her goal. She chewed her lip as she went back to her dresser. Was she selling out?

Before she left Parker's office and made a complete fool of herself in the elevator, Parker had promised that he would give her more complex stories if she would just go with Liam and cover this story. Now, standing in her room, it felt more like a bribe. Did Parker see her as a good journalist, or as someone he could push around? Groaning, she flopped onto her bed. She was a sellout.

"Oh, no. What's the matter now?" Bridget asked.

Madeline rolled to her back. "I'm a sellout, aren't I?"

Bridget joined her, and they both stared up at the popcorn ceiling with a few too many unknown stains. "You're going to the romantic wilderness with a tall, dark, and handsome billionaire. If that's selling out, then I'd sell out."

Madeline wrapped her arms around her stomach. Her

emotions were a wreck. "But, it goes against everything I've fought so hard for."

"Ugh, not that ridiculous oath you made yourself take."

Madeline flipped to her side. "It's an important oath."

"It's fake, Mad."

Madeline closed her eyes and took a deep breath.

Bridget sighed as she sat up. "So, make this story something you'd be willing to fight for. That wouldn't conflict with your oath. Not everyone is evil. Not everyone is Brett."

Stomach acid rose in Madeline's throat at the mention of her ex-fiancé. She hated that even his name caused her to feel sick. "Ugh, Bri. Why did you have to bring him up?" Rolling off the bed, she stood. Just thinking about him sent her emotions into turmoil.

"Because you have to move on," Bridget said, dropping down to her elbow and drawing circles around on Madeline's comforter with her finger. "Maybe Mr. *Davenport* is the way to do it." She wiggled her eyebrows.

"I've moved on." Madeline grabbed a few T-shirts from her closet and shoved them into her suitcase.

When she turned around, Bridget was staring at her. "You have not."

"I've totally moved on."

"Hmm." Bridget turned and zeroed in on Madeline's night-stand. "Jury, I would like to enter Exhibit A into evidence," she said, reaching for the drawer. The exact drawer where Madeline had stashed the photo of her and Brett that she couldn't quite bring herself to throw away.

"Wait!" she said as she lunged for the stand, but Bridget was faster.

"What do we have here?" Bridget asked, waving the picture in front of her.

"I was going to get rid of that."

Bridget titled her head. "Really?"

Madeline's mouth dried. "Yes." Dang, why didn't she sound more confident?

Bridget's gaze drifted from the picture and over to Madeline. "So you won't mind if I burned it? It could help rid you of the bad juju in your aura." She narrowed her eyes as if she was studying the air around Madeline.

"No, I wouldn't mind," Madeline said with a bit too much force.

Somewhere deep inside of her heart, she wasn't quite ready to shut that door. Brett might come back. He said he needed space to find himself, and once he did, she'd be waiting. She swallowed. But there was no way she'd let Bridget know she was holding on to that hope.

Bridget slipped the photo into her suitcase. "Here. Take it with you. Perhaps, you'll find the courage to throw it away while in Alaska." She gave Madeline a pointed look and then yawned. "I'm going to take a shower. My shift starts in a half an hour. If I don't see you tomorrow morning"—she pulled her into a hug—"have a safe flight."

Madeline nodded into her shoulder as she returned the hug.

Bridget pulled away. "And have some fun."

Madeline straightened her face. "This is for work, Bri."

She rolled her eyes and headed toward the door. "If I can't get the billionaire, I'd want him to go to you. Life isn't only about work. It'll pass you by if you're not careful!" she called from down the hall.

Madeline sighed and turned back to her luggage. Brett's photo stared back at her. She rubbed her hands on her pant legs as she contemplated taking it out. Then the image of Bridget hosting a séance while she was gone raced through her mind. Throwing her suit coat into the suitcase to cover it, she groaned. When had her life become such a complicated mess?

CHAPTER THREE

LIAM

*D*arkness surrounded Liam as he laid in bed, staring up at the smooth ceiling. Glancing over to his clock, he groaned. It was four in the morning, and he couldn't sleep. His mind just wouldn't shut off.

He shifted in his silk sheets and flipped to his stomach. One more hour before he needed to be up. One more hour before the damage control took place. One more hour before the whole world knew what a horrible man his father had been.

He scrubbed his face with his hands. There was no running now. Too many people's livelihoods depended on him. Families forever changed if he couldn't fix this. His chest constricted as he sat up. He needed a hot shower.

Slipping off the covers, he swung his legs over the side of his bed and stood. The warmth of his heated floors raced up his legs and settled in his stomach. Anywhere else, the cool fall weather would have affected people's lives. Not when you're a Davenport. He twitched as he made his way over to the adjoining bathroom.

He missed the way the outdoors grounded him. All this fancy stuff wasn't him—it was his father.

As he stared into the massive mirror that hung in the bathroom, his jaw clenched. One thing he knew for certain was, he was not his father and he would never be his father. No matter how much his new lifestyle wanted him to change.

Turning on the shower, he stepped into the enclosure. The water hit him from all sides.

Living in remote areas had taught him to take quick showers. Ice-cold water would do that to a man. No time to stand there and think when your body temperature was rapidly dropping.

In less than three minutes he was washed. He glanced around. What was he supposed to do now?

The Italian marble walls glistened under the droplets of water. An entire minivan could have fit in this shower. A wave of heat rushed over him. He needed to get out. Reaching over, he shut off the water and grabbed a nearby towel. Once he was dry, he wrapped it around his waist and stepped out.

While he brushed his teeth, he inspected his stubble. Alice would most likely tsk-tsk him for keeping his facial hair, but Liam didn't care. It was his last stance against the change he was forced to make. The only semblance of his past life he could keep. And, darn it, he'd keep it.

In his room, he dressed. It wasn't in his standard cargo shorts and T-shirt. This time, it was in the pressed European blue suit that Alice said made him look less intimidating—and less like a hobo.

Even though the suit was made from the finest fabrics, it scratched his skin. The collar felt as if it would strangle him, and the tie hung heavy around his neck. After slipping on his black polished shoes, he stood. Four forty-five. He still had fifteen minutes until Alice would be at the door. Fifteen minutes to be himself.

He grabbed his duffel bag he'd stashed in his closet and threw it onto his bed. Alice had informed him yesterday that the maid had already packed his suitcase and it was sitting in the foyer, ready to go. He scoffed as he grabbed his pants and sweatshirts. There was no way he was going to go to Alaska and not be comfortable.

After packing his clothes, he located all his outdoor gear and shoved them on top. He'd find a time to sneak away and do some rock climbing. Maybe even some camping. He wasn't expected to be the CEO of Davenport Outdoors all the time. Right?

He tucked his hiking boots on top and pulled the zipper closed. Shaking his head, he shouldered the bag and opened his door. He wasn't going to think about what was expected of him at this moment. It only made him feel as if a six-hundred-pound grizzly were sitting on his chest.

He clenched his fists. Right now, he needed to focus on getting to and from Alaska safely. After that, well . . . he'd figure something out.

The soft sound of a TV carried down the hall as Liam made his way toward the kitchen. He paused and slipped his duffel bag off his shoulder and dropped it next to the door. Georgia, his cook, was sitting at the counter peeling apples. Her gray hair was pulled up into a bun, and every so often, she reached up to adjust the readers she had perched on her nose. She was watching the news on the small television next to her.

"You're up early," Liam said as he walked into the room.

"Ah!" she screamed, wielding the paring knife in his direction.

Liam held his hands up.

"Oh, Mr. Davenport, you scared me." She laid her hand on her chest as her cheeks flushed. She glanced toward the clock then back to him. "Well, the apple fritters aren't going to fry themselves." Then her gaze turned curious. "It's only ten till. What are you doing up?"

Liam pushed his hands through his hair and headed over to the fridge. "I couldn't sleep."

Georgia nodded as she returned her focus to the apple in her hand. "Nervous for the flight?" she asked. "I wouldn't blame you if you were. I prefer my feet to stay on the ground."

Liam smiled as he pulled a jug of orange juice out and grabbed a glass.

"That's fresh squeezed," she said, nodding toward the pitcher.

"You work too hard." He gave her a pointed look as he poured.

She laughed. It was a melodious and soulful sound. "Well, I'll rest when I'm dead."

Liam leaned against the counter and smiled, allowing the familiarity those who had help raise him wash over his nerves. Being around them did help make this transition a bit easier. "How's Peter nowadays?" he asked.

Georgia placed the apple on the tray in front of her and started on the next one. "He's in Florida now. Got himself a girl." She held out her crossed fingers as she tilted her head up. "I'm hoping this is the one. I want me some grandbabies." She grinned at him.

He reached over and grabbed the apple she'd just peeled. Before she could protest, he took a bite.

She narrowed her eyes at him. "Liam Richard Davenport, just cause you're twenty-eight, doesn't mean I can't physically kick you from my kitchen."

He grinned as he tried to keep the apple juices from seeping from his lips. "Love you, too, Georgia."

She harrumphed and returned to the apple in her hand. "Davenports," she muttered.

Liam threw the core into the garbage just as Alice walked into the room. She had on a pressed suit, and her hair was pulled up into a bun. She looked the part of a high-power executive. Why didn't he?

"Good to see you're up," she said as she filled a mug with coffee. "And dressed in something presentable."

Liam tugged at his collar and nodded.

Before she could say anything further, the camera on the television screen flashed to a female reporter sitting at a desk. A tense cloud settled in the kitchen.

"More news on the Davenport family. This time, things aren't looking so good. Information has just been released that Richard Davenport, the late CEO of Davenport Outdoors, was involved with illegal poaching of endangered animals."

The reporter shuffled the stack of papers in front of her.

"Just how deep into the company do these indiscretions go? And were political officials paid to keep quiet? Find out first on Seattle Morning News, after these messages."

The reporter was replaced by a singing chicken.

Liam swallowed as anger built up inside of him.

"Whoa," Georgia said, breaking the silence and glancing over at him.

Alice rested her hand on his arm. "We can handle this. Just stick to the plan." She gave him a small smile.

The plan. Right. They had a plan. Liam finished the rest of the juice and set the glass in the sink. His stomach flipped. Why didn't those words make him feel any better?

Alice's phone rang drawing her into the hallway. Liam pulled open the cupboard and grabbed a cookie from the stash that he knew Georgia always kept in the back.

Alice returned before he finished it. Her face was contorted into a look of concern.

"What's wrong?"

She mustered a smile. "That was the DA. Apparently, your father is accused of extortion and using company property to store the animals he hunted." She swallowed as she paled. "I need to meet with the DA. You're going to need to go to Alaska without me."

"What?" Liam stared at her. She was the brains behind the whole PR plan. "I can't do this without you."

Alice shook her head. "I have to stay here." She made her way to the kitchen door. "You can do this, Liam. I know you can." She gave him another small smile and slipped out of the room.

"It's never calm in the Davenport house," Georgia muttered under her breath as she grabbed another apple.

Frustrated, Liam headed over to the door where he'd dropped his duffel bag earlier. At least now he didn't have to worry about trying to hide it from Alice. He was free to do whatever he pleased. But at this moment, that wasn't the kind of freedom he wanted.

MADELINE

As Madeline weaved in and out of the crowd at Sea-Tac airport, she came to only one conclusion—too many people traveled. She contemplated standing on a chair and telling everyone to go home but decided against it. It would probably draw too much attention from the security guards that stood about every ten feet.

Pulling her luggage closer to her, she sidestepped a particularly angry toddler who was flailing his legs and screaming. She shot the mom a sympathetic smile as she passed.

Madeline heels clicked on the tile as she walked next to the ticketing counters. Liam had said to meet at the airport at six, but he didn't say where.

Not sure what to do, she made her way over to one of the security guards that was standing next to the slow-moving line of people. He had his arms folded.

"Excuse me," she said, smiling. "I'm supposed to be meeting Liam Davenport here. Do you know where I might find him?" Now that she said the words out loud, she sounded ridiculous. How many people were there in Seattle? And she was expecting this guard to know a specific one?

The guard eyed her. "Who?"

"Liam Davenport."

The man's face grew red. "Did you say Davenport?"

Madeline took a step back. She wasn't sure why Liam's last name would cause such an angry reaction from this man. Disgusted, she understood. But angry? "Yes."

"From Davenport Outdoors?" A vein bulged from the man's neck.

It seemed best to try to calm the man down and then engage him in conversation. After all, Parker had been pretty clear—make the Davenports look good. "Listen, I'm not sure what you have against the Davenports—"

The guard laughed. "Oh, it's not just me. They're a terrible family. They think the rules don't apply to them. I'm an upstanding hunter. People like their kind make me sick." He stared down at her with fury in his gaze.

"I understand, but—"

"You're telling me you think it's okay that his dad has been poaching animals *illegally* and paying people off to keep it quiet? What kind of person are you?" His eyes narrowed. "I'd like to see some identification."

Madeline fumbled with her purse. "I'm not with the Davenports. I'm just a journalist." She pulled out her wallet and handed over her driver's license.

The guard took it and stared at it. Then he glanced up at her. "Madeline Abernathy?" he asked, but it sounded more like a statement.

She nodded.

The seconds that ticked by felt like hours. Finally, he sighed. It seemed that he'd taken that moment to calm his frustrations. He shoved her ID back in her direction.

"I'm guessing since he's a big moneymaker, he's not riding the commercial flights."

Madeline's heart sank. Why hadn't she thought of that? What was she supposed to do now?

He sighed. "Private hangars are in the south ramp. After the main terminal."

She peered out the sliding doors. "Outside?"

"Yep."

"Huh." How was she supposed to get there?

"Good luck," he said as he pushed off the wall. He started walking toward the line of people before he stopped and faced her again. "I'd do research about those you agree to do business with. People like the Davenports don't care about the little people. Guard yourself." He gave her a pointed look and then turned back around and disappeared into the crowd.

Madeline watched him fade from her view. A lump formed in her throat. What exactly had happened to this family? This man seemed extremely upset. But he was right. She couldn't call herself a journalist if she didn't do her research first.

She walked through the sliding doors and out into the drop-off area. Peering in both directions, she sighed. Pulling her purse from her shoulder, she rifled around until she found her phone. Just as she swiped it on, it rang.

She didn't recognize the number, but answered it anyway. "Hello?"

"Ms. Abernathy?" Liam's voice was icy.

"Yes."

"Where are you?"

"At the terminal."

His sigh was deep. As if her words grated on his nerves. "Commercial?"

"Yes."

"Why would you go there?"

Heat crept up her neck. "You never told me where I needed to be. When someone asks you to meet them at the airport, that's where you go."

"I understand that. It's just that now I have to send my driver to pick you up. It's putting us a whole half an hour behind." Annoyance filled his voice.

"Well, next time, be more specific." She wasn't going to let this man get her goat. She'd stand up for herself.

He was silent.

"*Hello?*" She made sure to add a bit of emphasis to the word.

"His name is Daniel. He'll be there in ten minutes. Be ready."

He hung up before she could offer a retort. She clenched her jaw as she dropped her phone into her pocket. After finding an empty spot on a bench, she sat down next to two elderly women.

She tried to seem busy, brushing down her pencil skirt, but the women's conversation piqued her interest.

"Poaching? Are you sure that's what they said?"

"Yes. Poaching. Can you believe that?"

Madeline tilted her head so she could hear better.

"What an awful person," the first woman replied.

From the corner of Madeline's eye, she saw the second woman nod. "They say he's been doing it for decades, but no one knew about it because he was paying people off to keep it quiet."

There was a scoff. "Rich people. Always thinking they can get away with anything. Always thinking their money is going to get them out of tough situations."

"Oh, and they say his son didn't know, but really? Like father, like son."

A black limo pulled up in front of her. Madeline's gaze whipped to it. It didn't feel like ten minutes had passed already.

A young guy in a suit got out of the driver's seat and rounded the hood.

"Are you Ms. Abernathy?" he asked as he zeroed in on her.

She stood. "Yes."

"Good. Mr. Davenport sent me. Ready?"

A gasp sounded behind her, causing heat to race to her cheeks. Grabbing the handle of her luggage, she charged toward the driver.

"Let's go," she said as he opened the door. All she wanted to do was disappear behind the tinted windows. As he pulled away from the curb, she glanced back. Both women had disgusted expressions as they stared at the limo.

She ducked down. Great. What had she gotten herself into?

CHAPTER FOUR

MADELINE

Once the limo was a good minute down the road, Madeline straightened. Anger flooded her body as the women's final words raced through her.

Did Liam know what his dad had done? Was she a fool to believe he had no clue? She shook her head. Of course he would lie. He was rich.

A wet sensation on her hand ripped her from her thoughts. She yelped and glanced around. Her breathing turned raspy as she stared into the face of the dog from the other day. He was seated in between the benches that ran parallel in front of her. The pounding of her heart beat in time with the thumping of his tail against the floor.

"W-Why is there a dog in here?" she called out, her voice cracking with each word.

As if speaking to it was the key to its release, the dog shot forward and stuck his face into Madeline's. She screamed and raised her hands. Ever since she'd been attacked by a German shepherd as a child, she was terrified of dogs. And that fear hadn't faded as she'd gotten older.

The dog's wet nose nuzzled her skin. She shivered as she pressed her back into the seat and debated flinging the door open and throwing herself from the moving vehicle.

"Um, help?" she whispered toward the driver. He was on the other side of the divide and didn't seem to notice her terror.

She took deep breaths as she slunk against the door. The dog didn't seem to want to bite her—which was a good sign. Mustering up some courage, she reached out and grasped the metal charm that hung from his neck. *DUKE* was stamped in large letters. He stared at her, causing her heart to race.

"Duke?" she whispered. Fear choking her voice.

He cocked his head to the side and then barked and leaned toward her.

She screamed as he lunged. But, instead of the sensation of a massive set of teeth ripping into her skin, the warm and wet feeling from earlier raced across her skin, paralyzing her. Duke placed his paws on both sides of her legs and climbed into her lap.

If she could have curled up into the fetal position, she would have, but the weight of his body crushed her legs, pinning her to the seat. She wiggled and jolted. Anything to get the massive dog off of her.

Liam's smug face flashed into her mind. She should have known he was behind this. Why did that insufferable man leave his dog in the limo? Who does that?

"Excuse me." She raised her voice, hoping to get the attention of the driver, but the dog's giant body and puffy hair absorbed her plea.

Before she slipped into hopelessness, the limo slowed to a stop. Duke remained on her lap, but he turned his attention to the movement on the other side of the window. The driver got out and made his way to her door. When he opened it, sunlight flooded the interior.

"Help," she squeaked.

"Duke!" the driver scolded.

"What did he do?" Madeline would recognize Liam's gruff voice anywhere.

"He's sitting on Ms. Abernathy."

Liam laughed. "Well, he is a good boy."

Madeline opened her lips to give that man a piece of her mind, but a whistle filled the silence.

"Come on, boy," Liam called.

Duke panted harder as he jumped from Madeline's lap and out the door.

She sat there, trying to compose herself. The smell of dog spit now surrounded her. She brushed at her cheeks, trying to remove the feeling of his tongue on her skin. A shudder ran down her spine.

Liam's figure filled the car's doorframe as he leaned down. "Well, are you coming?"

She sat there, staring at him. "You sent your dog to pick me up?"

He shrugged. "Daniel was bringing Duke to me. I figured you two would get along."

She stared at him. "You didn't think that would be inappropriate?" She thought about telling him she had a crippling fear of dogs, but stopped herself. There was no need to give this man more ammo against her.

"No," he said.

Madeline clenched her jaw. The words *rules don't apply to them* raced through her mind. She was doing him a favor, and how did he treat her? At the same level as his dog.

"If you're done freaking out now, the plane is waiting." Liam pushed away from the limo.

Madeline took a deep breath and stifled the thoughts that threatened to emerge. Being a journalist meant she could come up with quippy retorts at a moment's notice, but this wasn't the time.

Parker would not be happy if she got fired from this assignment. From the look on his face yesterday, things weren't going as well as the magazine was portraying. There had been desperation and worry in Parker's voice.

She grumbled her thoughts under her breath as she slid across the seat to the open door and stepped out.

Daniel had brought her to a small airplane hangar where a jet was parked. The side door was open, and a set of stairs rested in front of it.

She moved to pull her luggage from the limo, but Daniel had already grabbed it and set it next to the door.

"Did you need some help?" he asked, nodding toward the suitcase and then over to the plane.

She grabbed the handle. "No. I think I can manage from here."

"Sounds good," he said, shooting her a smile.

She returned it. Finally, the only person in Liam Davenport's world that treated her like a human being, and he was the hired help. Alice had all but turned her nose up at her, and Liam seemed more preoccupied with creatures on four legs than anyone around him.

"Are you coming?" she asked Daniel, waving toward the plane.

He grinned. "Nah. I've gotta stay here. I still drive Ms. Pickering around."

Madeline stared at him.

"Alice," he corrected.

She leaned forward. "I'm sorry."

Daniel gave her a confused look and then shook his head. "Oh, no. The Davenports have always been good to me."

Madeline eyed him but didn't push it further. The Davenports didn't care about anyone but themselves. This was evident in the recent discoveries made about Richard Davenport.

As she headed toward the stairs, the starting line of her article began swirling around in her mind: To the Davenport family, rules don't seem to apply.

LIAM

Duke barked and raced around Liam as he walked around the plane, doing his preflight check. There was something about Ms. Abernathy that had him rattled. He wasn't sure what it was, but Duke's incessant need to bark at him wasn't helping him sort out his thoughts.

He reached down and patted Duke's head. "Quiet, boy. I need to concentrate," he said.

When he rounded the plane, he caught a glimpse of Ms. Abernathy and Daniel. They were talking and smiling. Seeing their joy annoyed him. But then, that feeling made him stop. What was wrong with him? The day had just begun and yet he was already crabby.

"I'm just finishing up my last inspection," he said, clearing his throat and nodding toward the plane.

Madeline stared at him. "You. You're the pilot?"

Liam grinned. This plane was his baby. It was his home away from home. A gift from his father on graduation day. Which was ironic because his father hated the fact he went to flight school instead of Harvard. *Davenports go to Harvard, Liam.* Even to this day, his dad's voice echoed in his ears.

But this wasn't the time to think about this father. No need to stir up those emotions as well. "Yep. Isn't she a beauty?" he said, laying his hand on the outside of the plane.

Madeline kept staring at him. "You're going to fly this to Alaska?"

Why was this so hard to believe? "Yes. I am a pilot. I went to and—before you ask—yes, I graduated from flight school."

Her cheeks reddened. It accentuated those blasted freckles.

She leaned toward Daniel. "Have you flown with him?"

Daniel smirked. "He's an excellent pilot."

Madeline stared at Liam and then back at the plane.

Having had enough of her doubt, Liam walked over and

grabbed the banister of the stairs and took them two at a time. "Let's go," he said as he stepped onto the plane.

The familiar sights and smells relaxed him. This was just what he needed. He sighed as he slipped off his suit coat and hung it on the back of one of the chairs.

A thumping from the entrance of the plane grew louder. Madeline emerged from the opening with her suitcase in hand and a disgruntled expression. Liam started to move to help her, but then shook his head. He doubted she'd even take his help if he offered it. And right now, he didn't want to be rejected by Madeline Abernathy.

Instead, he turned and grabbed a bottle of water from the mini fridge.

"Where do I sit?" she asked.

He turned to see her glancing around.

"Pick a seat. Any seat."

She eyed him. Then walked over the chair furthest from him. "Do you do all the flying? Or do you have a copilot?"

Liam glanced at her. Did he detect the sound of hope in her voice? He nodded toward the cockpit.

"It's just me and Duke."

Duke barked.

"You're dog's your copilot?"

"Best one around."

She scoffed. "Figures you wouldn't care about the FAA. You feel you're above rules," she said under her breath.

Liam stopped and stared at her. "What?"

She looked over at him. "What?"

"What do you mean that I'm above the rules?"

She pinched her lips shut.

Frustration boiled up inside of him. She'd seen the news. Well, he should have expected that. "Maybe you should try asking questions and learning the truth before you assume, Ms. Abernathy," he said.

She furrowed her brow as she leaned against the back of the chair. "You're telling me that you'd tell me the truth?"

He took a step forward until he was inches from her. There was nothing he hated more than people who assumed things about him. He wasn't his father, and he wasn't his father's past. "You'll find I'm more accommodating when you ask." His voice came out lower than intended.

"How am I supposed to believe that you'd be honest?"

"I'm sure you have feelings about me and my family. But your judgment is not what I'm paying your magazine for. Get over yourself and do your job." He pushed away from her and headed toward the cockpit. His muscles tightened. Who was she to make these types of judgments about him? She didn't know him.

"Excuse me?" she almost shouted as she followed him. "Mr. Davenport, this isn't about making judgments. This is about right and wrong."

His gaze snapped to her. "And you're the expert on right and wrong?"

"I would like to think that people pay me to be an expert. It's a journalist's job."

Liam snorted as he turned and started to get everything ready for the flight. He'd seen their magazine. He knew they were in trouble. Alice thought that Davenport Outdoors was sure to get a feature article if they offered *The Journal* a substantial amount of money. Madeline seemed pretty haughty with the articles they'd been pumping out. "Seven ways to please your man? You're an expert on that?" He eyed her.

"Those aren't my articles," she said, leaning back and folding her arms. He could tell he was rattling her. Her cheeks were bright pink.

He forced a laugh. All journalists were the same. Self-righteous and full of themselves. "Sure. We'll go with that."

"And what about you? Claiming to love the outdoors, but secretly hunting animals *illegally* with your father?"

His chest constricted from the mention of his dad. He whipped around and glared at her. "Don't talk like you know me or my father."

Her eyes widened for a moment, but then she folded her arms. "All billionaires are the same."

"Yeah? Well, all *reporters* are the same."

She opened her mouth, and he could see the word *journalist* form on her lips. But Daniel appeared from behind her and raised his hand.

"Daniel, come in. Please," Liam said as he glared at Madeline and stepped past her and into the rest of the plane.

"I'm so sorry to interrupt, but Alice called you on my phone. It seems as if she can't get ahold of you?" Daniel handed his phone over to Liam.

Liam took it and headed out to the stairs. "Hello?"

"Liam?"

"Yeah."

"What's going on? Why haven't you answered my calls?"

"Relax, Alice. I'm just getting the plane ready. Ms. Abernathy and I are leaving in less than twenty minutes."

She was quiet for a moment. "Daniel said he heard you two arguing. Are you arguing with Ms. Abernathy?"

"No."

Alice sighed. "Stop arguing with her. We need her to write a positive article."

Liam rolled his shoulders. Alice wanted him to play nice, huh? But Madeline Abernathy was just so . . . infuriating. He took a deep breath. "Okay."

"Good. Now, call me as soon as you land in Alaska. We've got lots to do."

"Yep." He ended the call and stepped into the plane. "Here, Daniel," he said as he handed him the phone.

Daniel took it and stuffed it into his suit pocket. "Well, I should go. I'll see you when you get back." He nodded and slipped from the plane.

The air fell silent as Liam gathered his thoughts. He didn't want to apologize to the frustrating woman in front of him. But, he knew that it was his duty now. Kissing up to people who held his future in their hands.

"Ms. Abernathy, I think we may have gotten off on the wrong foot."

She scoffed as she looked over at him.

Frustration built up inside him, but he breathed it out. "Can we just move forward?"

She studied him. He twitched under her scrutiny. Finally, she sighed and straightened. "Let's move forward," she said, reaching out her hand.

Liam glanced at it and then met her gesture. Tiny sparks shot up his arm from the feel of her skin. It took all his energy not to pull away.

When the acceptable amount of time had passed, he dropped her hand. "We should get moving."

A look flashed over her face, and for a moment, it seemed as if she might have felt something too. Liam shook his head. He was being ridiculous. There were no feelings between the two of them.

Glancing at his watch, he let out a whistle. Duke came thundering up the stairs. "Time to go, buddy," he said as he patted his dog on the head. Duke turned and started licking Liam's hand.

Liam straightened and finished prepping the plane for takeoff. Madeline's words floated around in his mind. The things she'd said about him and his father—they soured his stomach. No matter how much he tried to push them out, they remained.

As he pulled the airplane door shut, he sighed. This was not what he wanted to be doing at this moment. He should have never allowed people into his life, even if she was here to help. Experience had taught him that when you're alone, you never get hurt. And Liam was determined to never get hurt again.

CHAPTER FIVE

MADELINE

*I*t didn't take long before the plane was ready and taxiing down the runway. At liftoff, Madeline clutched the armrests for dear life. She was knowingly putting her life in Liam Davenport's hands. What was she thinking?

It took a few of the breathing exercises she'd learned at the yoga studio—trips taken at Bridget's insistence—to calm her nerves. It didn't help that her argument with Liam kept resurfacing in her thoughts. Man, he really got under her skin with his pretentious ideas and sexy forearms.

She shook her head. That was not what she should be thinking about. He was a stuck-up and rude billionaire. But, the image of his muscular arms under his white shirt kept creeping its way back into her mind.

She rubbed her eyes as she scolded herself. She was not going to turn into that flighty, swooning girl that guys like Liam attracted. She was better than that.

Reclining her chair, she leaned her head back. It did help that the interior of plane was more spacious than flying in overbooked coach.

Traveling with a rich guy did have its perks. The seats were a soft leather and somehow magically adjusted to her body temperature.

Next to her was a small couch. And toward the back was a kitchenette. So much luxury for one man. She scoffed. She doubted he even knew what it was like to live like the ninety-nine percent.

When they reached cruising altitude, everything seemed calm. Which wasn't good. It was in these moments that her mind would start racing, and she wasn't looking forward to Liam Davenport being the topic of her thoughts. She glanced around, desperate for a distraction. Finally, she remembered the half-finished novel in her purse and settled in. Soon, she was whisked away into a magical world where rich men weren't pigheaded jerks.

It wasn't until the plane jolted, tossing her to one side, that she pulled herself from the story.

Folding over the edge of the page, she glanced around. She'd been so engrossed in her book that she hadn't noticed the darkness that crept in around her. Rain splattered across the windows as she peered outside. The clouds were thick and gray.

She unbuckled and stood, grabbing onto the wall next to her as she made her way to the cockpit. The plane tilted from side to side, forcing her to grasp onto anything she could find.

Liam's back was to her. He had his headset held up to his ear, and he was speaking into the mouthpiece. Madeline's ears were fuzzy from the sudden change in pressure. She had to swallow a few times to finally hear what he was saying.

" . . . sudden storm. What's the weather look like farther out?"

There was static and then she heard a muffled voice come through the headset. "Be—vised—mass—orm—"

Liam waited until the voice stopped before bringing the mouthpiece closer to his lips. "You broke up. Please repeat."

There was more static, followed by a broken voice.

Fear settled in Madeline's chest. "Liam? What's happening?"

As if he'd forgotten he wasn't alone, he jumped, whipping his gaze to her. "You need to get back in your seat and buckle up," he said, returning his attention forward.

"But—"

"No time to explain," he said as he focused on the controls in front of him. "There's a bad storm, and I—"

He stopped as he stared out the window. Madeline followed his gaze. A bright light shot across the sky, lighting up what looked like a dark cloud in front of them. The cloud moved and shifted against the sky. They looked like . . . birds. And they were headed straight toward them.

"Seat! Now!" Liam bellowed as he grasped onto the yoke and the plane jolted in response.

Madeline raced back to her chair. It was difficult to keep her body upright with how much the plane was jerking back and forth. Once she made it to her seat, she buckled in. Staring out the window, she tried to calm her pounding heart.

But the sight of birds surrounding the plane sent her heart racing. Suddenly, smoke billowed from the engine over the left wing, and then the right.

The plane shook. She ducked down and clutched her head in her hands. It seemed prudent to pray. Why was she here? What'd she gotten herself into? Her tiny apartment and menial stories didn't seem so bad right now.

Her stomach felt as if it had left her body as a deafening crack sounded and the plane began to fall. An oxygen mask tumbled down from the ceiling. Madeline grasped it and shoved it over her face. Taking deep breaths, she tried to calm her body. Nerves raced through her muscles and settled in her gut.

"Mayday! Mayday!" Liam's frantic voice echoed in her ears.

This was it. This was how she was going to die. She closed her eyes as a roaring sound took over her every sense. She tucked her head down until it almost touched her knees. Only a few more seconds, then this would all be over. Only a few more seconds, then she'd be dead.

A scream pierced the air. It took a moment for her to realize that the sound was coming from her lips. Then all thoughts disappeared from her mind as the sound of her terror was replaced by crunching metal.

Out of instinct, she sat up. Debris from inside the plane flew toward her, smacking her in the forehead and sending her body flying to the left.

She moaned as her eyesight grew blurry and her body turned limp. She tried to fight it, but eventually she slipped into the darkness that surrounded her.

LIAM

Liam's ears rang as he groaned and peeled open his eyelids. Blinking over and over again seemed to help clear his cloudy sight. Red lights on the dash flashed. A piercing sound filled the air. Liam reached up and cradled his head. What had just happened?

He looked out the windows. Whiteness surrounded him. The mountain slope. He'd noticed it when he had to bring the plane down after both engines died. It took all his schooling to calm himself down and glide the plane onto the snow. He winced as he recalled the sound of metal smashing into the ground.

His arms and legs ached, but he braved the pain and sat up. Where were Duke and Madeline? His heart surged at the thought of them injured—or worse. His fingers fumbled to unbuckle the seat belt.

"Duke? Madeline?" he called out and then instantly regretted it. Reaching down, he touched his stomach. He pulled his fingers away and cringed. There was no blood, but his ribs ached. He wondered if he had bruised a few of them.

After taking a few deep breaths, he pulled his body from the chair and staggered toward the back of the plane.

"Madeline?" he called out again.

Her panicked expression raced through his mind. He'd been desperately trying to reach anyone on his radio that he hadn't had time to discuss with her what was happening to them. For a moment, the thought that she hadn't been able to buckle into her seat caused his stomach to tighten.

He grasped the wall of the plane. His legs felt like Jell-O. Every muscle ached. He wasn't sure where they were, or if they were safe. But at least he was alive.

A whimper, followed by a wet feeling on his fingers, shocked his system. Liam's heart stuttered as he glanced down. Duke was next to him with his face inches from Liam's hand. He panted and then leaned forward and licked Liam again.

"Hey, boy," Liam rasped as he reached out and patted Duke's head. His throat was raw, and he winced as the words struggle to come out.

Duke whimpered again and nuzzled his hand.

"It's okay. I'm okay. I just need a minute," he said. He rested his shoulder against the wall of the plane as he took as deep of a breath as his injury would allow.

That seemed to appease the dog. His tongue hung from his mouth as he panted next to Liam.

After a few seconds, Liam waved to Duke. "Come on, boy. Let's go find Ms. Abernathy." He stood and made his way into the back.

When he located Madeline, relief and fear rushed through him causing him to shake. He sucked in his breath as he took in her condition. She was slumped over in her seat with a small gash across her forehead. Her eyes were closed, and she was so still. His heart pounded as he reached out and pressed his fingers on her throat.

A hand grasped his arm as her eyes whipped open. She stared at him and parted her lips. If his head hadn't been aching before, the high-pitched scream that she released would have done the job.

"Ms. Abernathy," Liam tried, but he could barely hear himself over her scream. "Ms. Abernathy!" he tried again.

She continued to scream.

Finally, he reached over and covered her mouth with his hand. That muffled the scream until it finally died out. Madeline's eyes remained open, and her gaze darted around the room.

"Ms. Abernathy, you're in shock, but you have to stop screaming." He paused. "I'm going to take my hand away. You're not going to start screaming again, are you?"

She stared at him with her gaze full of fear. For a moment, his heart went out to her. She must be so terrified.

When she shook her head, he pulled his hand away.

She straightened as she looked around. "W-What happened?"

Liam collapsed in the chair next to her, and the adrenaline that pumped through his veins lessened, causing his body to shiver. "The plane hit that flock of birds. They destroyed the engines, and I had to land in the mountains."

Her face paled as she peered out the windows and then back to him. "Are you okay?" she stammered.

He shrugged, ignoring the stabbing pain that shot through his stomach. "I'll be fine."

Liam saw a shudder race through her body as she turned to face him. Her countenance had changed as if reality had finally settled around her. "What did you do?" she whispered as she glared at him.

All the sympathy he'd felt for her earlier disappeared. "Excuse me?"

She straightened in her chair as he cheeks reddened. On any other day, he would've thought she looked adorable, but the fury that spewed from her gaze changed his feelings.

"What did you do?" she repeated as she struggled to stand.

Liam tried to keep his voice calm "What did *I* do? Do you

think I wanted this? That I purposefully called on Zeus to create this storm that got us into this mess?"

Madeline teetered as she stood next to her seat. Her hand flew out to steady herself. "I should have known better than to get into a plane with a party boy. After what you did to your dad's yacht . . ." She glared at him.

He raised his hand. There was no way he was going to let her stand there and talk about things she knew nothing about. "I suggest you stop talking right now. You don't know me."

She hardened her gaze. "Oh, I think I know just enough about you."

Heat pricked at his neck. "From the *news*?" He quoted the air. "What a joke. I have yet to meet a reporter who actually cares about facts and not selling magazines."

Madeline stepped toward him and opened her lips. Before she could say anything, Duke bounded over to her and began licking her hand. She jerked it away and looked as if she was contemplating climbing onto the chair to get away from the dog.

Liam straightened, grateful for the break in the conversation. He wasn't interested in fighting anymore. He needed to find out where they were and come up with a plan. "I'm done arguing," he said as he headed over to the door. He needed to find out if the plane was in a safe location and if the emergency location transmitter had survived the crash.

"Wait," Madeline said, as she rushed after him.

Liam ignored the panic in her voice as he pulled the latch and shoved the door hard with his shoulder. Cold wind raced around him as he glanced out. Snow surrounded them. He leaned out. Half of the plane was buried in white powder, but from the look of things, it didn't seem like they were in any imminent danger. The plane seemed to be securely parked on the mountain slope. But, from where he stood, he couldn't make out the condition of anything else.

When he turned back around, he saw Madeline's wide eyes.

"What?" he asked as he shut the door to keep what little heat they had inside of the plane.

Her cheeks reddened. "I thought you were leaving me," she said.

Liam fought a laugh. She annoyed him—that was true—but he'd never leave her. He made his way past her, making sure to pause when he was inches away. "Trust me, I thought about it," he said as he glanced down at her. He saw her shiver and, inside, he smiled.

He made his way to the back where he located his duffel back and the suitcase the maid had packed. First thing they needed to do was to find warm clothes. The plane offered protection against the wind, but without electricity, heat was a no-go.

"Grab your suitcase," he said, nodding in her direction.

She made her way over to her bag and grabbed its handle. "Okay?"

He glanced over to her. Was he going to have to walk her through everything? "Now open it and find something to wear. It won't take long before this plane becomes a metal coffin. The temperatures drop rapidly around here." He waved to her pencil skirt and heels. "Not really attire to keep a person warm."

She unzipped her suitcase and rifled around. Liam grabbed out his hiking gear from the top of his duffel bag. Then he pulled out his sweatshirt and jeans. There was no way he was going to wear a suit in Alaska.

He turned to see that Madeline was still standing by her suitcase, staring into it.

"What's wrong?" he asked, walking over to her.

She glanced at him. "I'm not sure what I have is wilderness appropriate."

He reached into her bag and began to pull out satin tank tops and fitted pencil skirts. Underneath were lacy underwear and bras. The image of Madeline wearing these items raced through his mind. Liam tried to calm his heart as it picked up speed.

He clenched his fists. *Get a grip, Liam,* he scolded himself.

Diverting his energy seemed like the best idea. "Why would you bring these things to Alaska?" He tried to keep the bite out of his tone, but Madeline seemed to pick up on it.

"I wasn't the one who—" She glanced over to him and snapped her lips closed. "Well, I guess I didn't think that I'd crash-land on a mountain." She stammered for a moment before she turned to meet his gaze head-on.

He was too distracted by her ridiculous choice in clothes to engage her. He shook his head as he pulled more items out. A picture floated to the ground. Glancing down at it, Liam picked it up. It was a snapshot of a good-looking guy with his arm wrapped around Madeline. For a moment, Liam allowed himself to wonder who he was.

He shook his head. What was wrong with him? There was no reason for him to even care about the details of Madeline's life. She was annoying and bossy. And irritated the crap out of him.

"Boyfriend?" he asked, handing the photo over to her.

She snatched it from him. "Yes," she mumbled.

There seemed more to the story then she was letting on, but he decided not to push it.

"Cool." He waved his hand toward her items. "None of these are going to work out there. Come here." He nodded toward his duffel bag.

She followed after him. He grabbed a flannel shirt and jeans, and he handed them to her as her eyebrows shot up.

"Really?" she asked.

"Really."

"Besides the fact that I'm completely insulted that you think you and I are the same size, I doubt your clothes would protect me anymore than my own will."

Liam stepped closer to her. He tried to ignore just how good she smelled. Like fresh sheets and summer nights. "Ms. Abernathy, with your skimpy clothing, you'll freeze in the Alaskan weather." As he leaned closer to her and deepened his voice, her eyes widened. Good. He wasn't going to be the only person uncomfortable here.

He peered into her bright green eyes. "Now, personally, I'd love to leave you here. But I have a feeling Parker wouldn't too happy about me abandoning his best reporter to fend for herself against bears and freezing temperatures." He pressed the clothes into her chest. "Now, be a good girl and put these on."

Her arm wrapped around the clothes as she glared at him. "Fine." She turned and headed toward the bathroom and shut the door.

Alone, Liam let out a sigh. He was going to have to watch himself around Madeline Abernathy. There was a fire in her gaze and a snap to her wit that seemed to be drawing him in. And that, he just could not have.

CHAPTER SIX

MADELINE

*M*adeline stood in front of the pile of clothes that she'd set down on the toilet seat. Her hands shook as she grasped them in front of her. She wasn't sure if it was from frustration with Liam or the fact that she'd just survived a plane crash. A plane crash that had been caused by Liam. He seemed to be the source of her problems. Period.

She glared at the door. Just who did that man think he was? She huffed as she grabbed the jeans he'd handed to her. A cocky, know-it-all pain in her butt—that's what he was.

She shook out his jeans, enjoying the snapping sound they made. Once she was out of her skirt, she slipped the pants on and prayed that they wouldn't fit. As she slid them up past her under-wear, she smiled. Thank goodness. There was a good ten inches between her stomach and the waistband.

After rolling the top a few times, the pants stayed up. She kept her satin tank top on but took off her suit jacket. She rolled her eyes. Bridget and her insistence on Madeline taking sexy things with her on this trip. She should have known better.

After Bridget had left the room for her shower, she reappeared stating she just couldn't let Madeline go anywhere with a billionaire and the ratty clothes she was packing. Before Madeline could stop her, Bridget had thrown out all of her sensible clothes and replaced them with—as Bridget put it—man-catching clothes. Of course, they consisted of sexy tops and pointless underwear.

Maybe she needed to start standing up to Bridget and her ridiculous ideas. At this moment, Madeline wished she had her sweatpants and NYU sweatshirt.

She was surprised at how soft Liam's flannel shirt was as she pulled it on. And it smelled—so good. She brought the fabric to her nose and inhaled. The scent of a man mixed with the woods filled her senses. Her heart raced as she imagined Liam wearing this exact shirt.

Then imaginary Liam shot her that cocky smile of his, and the picture soured. If only he wasn't such a jerk, maybe she'd allow herself to be attracted to him.

Ha. What a joke. He was a billionaire. Having a higher sense of superiority came with the territory. It was, like, a requirement. They didn't give you that last dollar, tipping you over to billionaire unless you had a level of haughtiness around you. And for Liam Davenport, humility was not in his repertoire.

Once the shirt was buttoned, she opened the door. Her face heated as she was met with the tanned back of Liam Davenport. His muscles moved as he swept his shirt around and pushed his arms into the sleeves.

He glanced back at her and grinned.

Crap. He'd seen her stare. She pinched her lips together and walked out. There was no way to redeem herself, so it was best to just act confident. Even if her insides were jumbled from his presence.

"See? These do not fit," she said, lifting up his shirt and waving to the waistband that she'd rolled.

He just nodded.

She stood there, glaring at him. Why did his half-smile and sparkle in his eye annoy her so much? He seemed to bring out the worst in her.

"And your clothes smell strange." Hmm. The thought seemed more like a zinger in her head. Now that it was spoken aloud, she felt like an idiot.

He kept watching her as his fingers worked their way down the buttons of his shirt. He nodded, feigning a look of understanding. "I'll let my housekeeper know. Can you describe the smell?"

She shoved her discarded clothes into her suitcase. "They smell like a man." Pinching her lips shut, she felt her cheeks heat as she glanced over to him.

"Well, I have no idea why they'd smell like that," he said as he pulled out a ball cap from his bag and placed it on his head.

She narrowed her eyes. "You know what I mean."

That half-smile was back. "I'll tell my housekeeper to make my clothes smell less like a man."

She let out an exasperated sigh. "You do that." There was no way she'd come back from that. No use in trying. She'd completely made a fool of herself. Twice. Man, she was on a roll.

There was something about Liam's presence that had her all shook up. It must be the shock of surviving a plane crash with him. That had to be it. She took a deep breath. She needed to get a grip. Now.

He slipped on his boots and stood. "So, I'm going to head out and check where we are and the condition of the plane. Hopefully, the tailboom-sited external antenna hasn't been damaged." He glanced over to her. "It's what connects to the emergency transmitter locator."

Madeline nodded as if she knew what he was talking about. "And if it's damaged?"

Liam's face paled for a moment. "If it is, then no one's coming for us. We're on our own. It's best that we stick around the plane.

At least for tonight. We do not want to get stuck outside without protection when the sun goes down." He glanced at his watch.

Madeline chewed her lip. Fear coursed through her veins. It was still taking her mind and her body time to realize that she was in a plane. A crashed plane.

"Do you think you could rustle up some grub?" he asked, nodding toward the kitchenette.

She glanced over to him. "I think so."

"It's not going to be much. Betty does a pretty good job cleaning my plane after every flight. For our sakes, let's hope she decided to slack this last time."

At the mention of Liam's maid, Madeline's lips tightened. Was that all she was to him? A person to do things for him? She wanted to tell him off, but chewed her cheek instead. Her life did depend on his know-how of the wilderness. Best not to provoke the billionaire until they were safely out of the mountain.

Liam went over to the far closet and pulled out a jacket. As he slipped it on, he smiled at her. It made her uncomfortable. And worried her. She took a step back. The symptoms of a concussion raced through her mind. He said he was all right. But was he?

LIAM

Liam zipped the front of his coat and turned to glance over at Madeline. She had a disgruntled look on her face. He shot her a smile again, hoping to help ease her pain.

She leaned down and caught his gaze. "You're smiling a whole lot. Should I be worried that you have a concussion?" She raised her finger. "Most people don't even show signs of a concussion. Are you confused? Are you more sensitive to light? What about sound?" She leaned in, studying his eyes.

"Ms. Abernathy," he said, backing away.

"Yes?"

"If I'm confused, do you think it's wise that you ask me this many questions?"

She glanced up at him with a sheepish expression. "I'm sorry. Useless information again." She tapped her forehead and then winced when she neared the gash on her head.

"Hey," he said as he stepped forward. "Let me help you with that." He reached out and grabbed her hand.

She stared at him. "I—um—"

"No excuses. I'm the cause of that." He guided her over to the chair and motioned for her to sit. She looked nervous but didn't protest.

He walked over to the sink on the other side of the plane and pulled open the cupboard door. He pushed the cleaning supplies and chemicals around until he found the first aid kit.

He grabbed a dishrag and water bottle from the fridge and walked back over. Her eyes widened as he knelt down in front of her.

"Here, hold this," he said, handing her the rag. He tried to ignore the fact that she was just inches from him.

She took it and began twisting it in her hands.

"Nervous, Ms. Abernathy?"

"Madeline."

He glanced over to her. For a moment, he felt lost in the depths of her green eyes. "Madeline," he said.

Her cheeks flushed as she nodded.

He opened the bottle and waved at her to hand him the dishrag. Once he wetted it, he began to dab around her cut. She winced and sucked in her breath. Being this close confused him. It was as if seeing the flecks of gold in her eyes or the highlight of red in her hair made her more human. It was easier to dislike her at a distance.

"You okay?" he asked, the deepness of his voice surprising even him.

She just nodded. He could tell she was avoiding his gaze as she swept it around the inside of the plane.

"What's the plan?" she asked and then winced as he neared her cut.

"Sorry," he said. She gave him a weak smile. "After we stay the night here, we'll head down the mountain and out of the snow line. Once we get our bearings, we'll head toward water. Water will lead us to the ocean. Hopefully, we'll see a boat or run into hunters." He doused the other end of the rag with water and finished cleaning her cut. "I've got good news," he said as he put the soiled towel down. "You're not going to need stitches."

She glanced over at him, and his heart quickened. There was something so unabashed by her stare, and it made him extremely uncomfortable.

"Would you even know how to do that?" she asked, eyeing him.

"Give you stitches?"

She nodded.

"I've done it a few times. Sometimes on myself. Sometimes on my buddies when they've been stupid."

A smile twitched on her lips as if she was recalling something funny.

Liam raised his brow. "What?"

He saw the tension drop from her shoulders. "Nothing."

"Not nothing. You smiled just now. And that, Madeline, is something I haven't seen you do."

Her mouth dropped open. "I smile."

Liam returned to the first aid kit and grabbed a Band-Aid. "Sure. We'll go with that." When he turned around, she had a giant grin plastered on her face.

"See?" she said through her clenched teeth as she pointed to her mouth.

"Seriously? You look like you belong on a jack-o-lantern."

Her expression softened as she glanced at him. A sadness surrounded the air. What had he said?

He pulled off the wrapper and leaned in. "Now, hold still," he said as he brought the bandage closer to her skin. Once it was secured, he dropped his hands and wiped his fingertips with his thumb, trying to get the feeling of her soft skin off of them. It wasn't working.

"How do I look?" she asked, striking a pose.

"Great," he said, and then instantly regretted it. Madeline glanced over at him with her eyes wide. "As good as anyone could who's just survived a plane crash could," he added.

"Hey, you should look at yourself." She swatted his arm as she stood and made her way into the bathroom where she studied herself in the mirror.

The weight that seemed to be crushing his chest lessened the farther she got. For a moment there, they'd almost gotten personal. He'd been tempted to talk about his feelings. He let his gaze fall to her. Could he do that? Actually have a positive relationship with a reporter?

Then all the negative articles that had been written about him crossed his mind. Lies and stories made up just to make a buck. He shook his head. No, he couldn't confide in Madeline. She'd just take his secrets and sell them to the highest bidder.

Besides, she didn't care about him. He was just a story for her. Another rung on her corporate ladder. And he couldn't ignore the fact that she had a boyfriend. Not that Liam cared. But it did help remind his heart and head that she was off-limits—no matter how disappointed that made him feel.

CHAPTER SEVEN

MADELINE

*M*adeline was alone. Scratch that. She was alone in the sense of there were no other humans. There was however, a dog. And he stank. Every time she moved inside the plane, Duke followed after her. She'd lost count of how many times she almost stumbled over him.

"Duke," she exclaimed for the thirty-third time. "Just go lie down." Why Liam refused to take him along on his scouting expedition was beyond her.

He'd been gone for ten minutes, and already Madeline had contemplated opening the door and shooing Duke out. But she'd promised Liam she'd keep an eye on the animal. She sighed. Why did she have to make promises that made her miserable? Next time, she really needed to think before she spoke.

Duke barked at her.

Shushing him, she moved to the small kitchenette. Liam asked her to put something together for dinner from the canned food in the kitchen. Hopefully, the rescue team would find them before tomorrow. If not . . . Madeline shook her head. She didn't want to think about that. They were going to be found. Period.

After opening and closing the cupboards, she laid out all the canned goods on the counter. All sorts of rich-people food stared back at her. What was she supposed to do with canned caviar and pickled asparagus? Her stomach twisted at the thought of eating either much less eating them together.

"You eat this?" she asked Duke who just cocked his head to the side. Every moment she spent with the furry animal seemed to help ease her fear of him. She didn't like him, but she was starting to tolerate him. Which was a step in the right direction. Especially since they needed to survive together.

Rifling around in the drawers, Madeline found a can opener. She made her way through the vegetables and on to the meat. When she opened the can of salmon, Duke perked up.

"Ah, so you do eat this," she said as she glanced down at him. "Did you know that every year, there are more than thirty-three million cases of food poisoning?"

Duke barked.

"I know. It's terrible." She grabbed a few plates and dished up the food. The colors were strange and the smells even stranger.

Liam appeared in the doorway of the plane. His cheeks were pink as he dusted off his jacket and kicked his boots against each other. He eyed her as he shut the door behind him. "What are you doing?" he asked.

"I'm making dinner." She paused. "Actually, I'm opening dinner."

Liam walked up to the counter and peered at the plates. "Did you open everything I had?"

"Well, not everything. I stayed away from pigeon pate? Seriously?"

Liam took it from her hand and smiled. "I got it from a girl—" He cleared his throat. "I got it in Paris."

Madeline eyed him. So, he had a girl in Paris. Interesting.

"Fine. You got this fancy food from girls you've met. It still doesn't explain why a billionaire's son is eating lasagna from a can." She picked up the can of Chef Boyardee and waved it in front of his nose.

"Would it blow your reporter mind to find out that I just might prefer this to the real thing?"

"Journalist. And yes. You could employ the finest chefs to personally cook for you whenever you want it, but this is what you choose?" She motioned toward the plates.

Liam's shoulders tightened. "That's not me." His voice was low. He turned away from her and made his way over to the small table sandwiched between two leather recliners.

Madeline's stomach twisted, and it wasn't from the smells coming from the food. She'd upset him, yet she wasn't sure how. Apparently, his dad's money wasn't a topic he liked to discuss.

As she watched him stare out the window, she contemplated what she should say, or if she should say anything at all. There were clearly some issues there. It would probably be better to keep things platonic between them. There was no need to try to get to know Liam Davenport. This was just a job. That was it.

Suddenly, Liam climbed up onto the chair and started kicking the window. Madeline stared. What was he doing? Was what she said that terrible?

"Liam?" she called out, walking closer to him.

He didn't stop. The window began cracking underneath the impact. Duke sat up and started barking.

"Liam!" she said as she reached out and grabbed his arm.

Once the window was gone, Liam turned. "What?"

"You're breaking the window."

He glanced back. "Yeah."

Madeline sighed and folded her arms. "Where I come from, that's not a normal way to deal with stress."

He studied her. "Stress?"

"Yes, stress. You know, from the plane crash, or your apparent desire not to talk about your dad's money."

Liam narrowed his eyes as if he didn't understand what she was saying. Then he nodded. "I was breaking the window so I can build a fire." He waved toward the opening. "It's to vent the smoke."

It was Madeline's turn to stare at him.

"Wait. You thought you made me so upset that I started breaking a window?" He chuckled under his breath.

That just made Madeline more frustrated. "Well, how was I supposed to know? After you walked away, saying you didn't want to talk about something, you start busting up your plane."

Liam stepped closer to her with that smug look back on his face. "Ms. Abernathy, don't flatter yourself. You irritate me, yes. But not as much as you seem to think." He leaned in, inches from her face.

She held her spot even though he made her insides burn with anger. How can one man make her so furious by just being close to her? She tried to think of a good comeback but was at a loss. Instead, she gave him one last look and then turned and walked over to the counter.

"Let's eat," she said as she grabbed the plates and set them on the table.

Liam nodded. "I'm going to start a fire first." He grabbed a metal bowl from one of the cupboards and set it in front of the window. Then, he grabbed some of the brush he'd brought in from outside and broke the sticks. After ripping up some paper towels, he stacked them in the bowl and lit the towels. A crackling sound filled the air as the sticks became engulfed in flames.

Warmth filled the cabin as Liam turned and joined her at the table. They ate in silence, both staring out to the vast white landscape next to them.

"Did you find anything? You know—outside?" she asked.

Liam sighed as he set his plate down and sat back. "Yeah. Looks like everything was destroyed."

A chill raced up Madeline's neck. "So, no one knows where we are?"

Liam shook his head. "From what I can tell, the storm most likely blew us west, but I'm not sure how much or even where that puts us."

Madeline pressed on her eyelids. Stranded. They were stranded. In the Alaskan wilderness. "Do you think anyone is coming to look for us?" She peered over to him.

He nodded. "Of course. I just wonder how successful they will be."

She swallowed. "How hard is it? Just send out a helicopter to look for us."

"It's not that easy. It's like looking for a needle in a haystack. There are millions of places we could have crashed. It's best for us to head down the mountain in the morning."

Madeline couldn't handle the anxiety that was coursing through her, so she stood and put that energy into pacing. "Leave the plane? What if they find it and we're not here? How much harder are we going to be to find if we're in the wilderness?"

The muscles in Liam's jaw tightened. "We can't risk staying here. What if they never find the plane?"

Her hands shook as she gripped the counter. It seemed that the stress and pressure from the entire day had come crashing down on her. The realization that they were stranded hit her hard. She might die with Liam Davenport being the last person she had spoken to.

She whipped her gaze over to him and glared. She should have never put her life in his hands.

He sighed. "What now, Ms. Abernathy?" He scrubbed his face with his hands.

She opened her lips to speak, but the words that she wanted to say didn't come out. Instead, "Ninety-four percent of aviation crashes occur in private planes," spilled from her lips.

Liam stood, scrunching his face and then releasing it. As if he were fighting the thoughts that were racing through his gaze. "Is that so?" He sighed as his shoulders slumped, and he made his way over to the couch. Opening the compartment above him, he removed a sleeping bag and pillow.

Madeline fiddled with the edges of her sleeves. She hadn't meant to make that sound like an accusation, but she feared it did. "Liam, I'm—"

He held up his hand. "Look. We're both exhausted and probably a bit shook up from what happened. Let's get a good night's sleep because we have a long day ahead of us." He waved to the couch. "You can sleep here, and I'll sleep on the floor."

"But—"

He turned to look at her, exasperation in his gaze.

"This is your plane," she whispered.

He shook out the sleeping bag out and let it float down onto the couch. Then he rifled around in the same compartment and emerged with a blanket. "It's called being a gentleman, Ms. Abernathy."

Great. She was back to being called *Ms. Abernathy*. Every time he said it, she felt like he was talking to her mother. But it didn't seem right to bring that up at this moment. From the looks of his downturned lips and slumped posture, he was tired.

"Okay," she said. If she were honest with herself, she was exhausted too. Sleep did sound better than arguing.

He nodded and then disappeared into the bathroom, leaving Madeline alone.

She wrapped her arms around her chest and glanced around. Why couldn't she just say the right things when she was around him? Why did he muddle up her brain every time he looked at her?

She shook her head. She wasn't going to allow herself to think anymore tonight. Pulling the covers back, she crawled underneath them. Tomorrow, her mind would clear. Tomorrow, things would be better.

LIAM

"Hey."

A harsh whisper and a hard shove to his shoulder pulled Liam from his dream. Or nightmare. They were becoming one in the same.

"What?" he asked, bolting up and glancing around.

Madeline's wide eyes peered over at him.

He pulled the blanket from him. If there was danger around, he couldn't afford to get tangled up in it. "Everything okay?" He blinked against the darkness, attempting to focus on Madeline.

For a moment, he thought he saw her lower lip quiver. His chest swelled at the thought of her feeling scared. The sudden urge to protect her raced through him.

"Hey. What's wrong?" he asked, reaching out to rest his hand on her knee. She had her legs drawn up to her chest, and she was hugging them.

Her face paled as she scooted closer to him. She didn't seem that panicked so there must not be any imminent danger. Adrenaline rushed through his body as he tried to relax it. He moved to lean against the couch, and Madeline followed him. He grabbed his blanket and draped it across their laps.

"Can I just sit next to you?" she asked.

Liam glanced over at her. Her jaw was set as she stared out into the darkness around them. "Sure," he said. Was it wrong that he enjoyed the feeling of her shoulder next to his? That for the first time since meeting her, she seemed vulnerable?

He shook his head. There was something clearly wrong with her. It felt wrong to enjoy the situation while she was in pain. *Focus on her,* he chanted in his mind.

"Do you want to talk about it?" He kept his voice calm as he glanced over at her.

She closed her eyes and shook her head. "Not really."

"Is it the crash? Are you scared? Cause, I won't let anything happen to y—us." It felt a bit too intimate to confess to her that he would take care of her specifically. Besides, she seemed to hold onto her independence with all of her strength. He didn't want to take that away from her.

"A little," she whispered.

"Trust me, I'm a bit scared as well. But we'll be fine. As long as we keep calm, we should be fine."

"That doesn't make me feel any better."

"What? That I'm scared?"

From the corner of his eye, he saw her nod.

"But, I thought that's what you women wanted. A man who wasn't afraid to show his feelings."

She scoffed. "That's for when we watch chick flicks, and you refuse to cry even though you're welling up inside. When we're stranded in the wilderness, we want to know there's nothing that will scare you." She inched closer to him.

Out of instinct, he wrapped his arm around her shoulders. Her posture tightened, but then relaxed. She rested her head on his arm. He leaned in until his lips were inches from her ear.

"There's nothing that scares me. I'm the scariest thing you'll ever come across."

He felt her shoulders rise and fall with her laughter.

"I believe you," she whispered. "Most billionaires are pretty scary."

Liam pulled back and studied her. A billionaire? Is that all she saw him as? Why couldn't people look past his father's wealth and define him as something else? Was this his curse?

He contemplated pulling away, but Madeline had already stilled. So, he stayed, but he couldn't stop the frustration boiling up inside. He leaned his head back on the couch behind him.

At least when he was on his own, most people had no idea who he was. He could melt into the crowd and become like everyone else. He was Liam Davenport and that was it. He wasn't Liam Davenport, heir of the Davenport Outdoors monopoly. And he preferred that anonymity.

He closed his eyes as a resolution rose up in his chest. Once this PR nightmare was taken care of and Davenport Outdoors was safe, he'd sell his shares and leave. Disappear into the world and never look back. There was nothing for him in Seattle.

Everyone that was supposed to love him was gone, and he was okay with that. It was as if the world was telling him that he was meant to be alone. It was time he started listening.

CHAPTER EIGHT

MADELINE

$\mathcal{M}$adeline shivered as her eyes fluttered open. She took in the bowl of glowing embers, Duke laying a few feet away, and the whiteness of the snow out the window. Crap. The plane crash hadn't been a nightmare. It was real. Which meant the arm wrapped around her right now belonged to none other than Liam Davenport. She could feel his chest rising and falling under her head. Her heart pounded in her ears.

She was sleeping on Liam. Why was she sleeping on him? What had she done last night?

She inched her body away from his. Once she was a good distance away, she bolted off the floor and into the bathroom as her mind struggled to keep up.

The click of the latch sent shivers up her back. Turning, she sat on the toilet lid in front of her. Once she was alone, she allowed her emotions to spill over. Her shoulders shook as the memories from her past flooded her mind.

She knew why she'd climbed into Liam Davenport's bed. She'd been so scared. Everything from her childhood that she'd attempted to lock away came spilling out. Every last horrible detail.

She stifled a sob as she turned her face toward the ceiling. Why couldn't she just be strong? Why did she allow what her father had done to her mother creep into her life? She chewed the inside of her cheek. She wasn't a little girl anymore, and reacting that way made her feel ridiculous.

But there was something about the complete helplessness she'd felt when the plane fell from the sky that uncovered past feelings. The emotions that would cause her to crawl under her bed as a little girl to escape the arguments of her parents. It was there that she would plug her ears and recite information that she had read earlier that day. Anything to drown out their fighting.

When her parents died in a car crash when she was sixteen, she thought she had resolved all her past feelings. Apparently, after the ridiculous display of panic she'd shown Liam, that wasn't the case. She was just as weak and scared as she had been as a child.

Wiping at her tears, she steadied her nerves. She needed to get over the past and move forward. Exposing her weaknesses to anyone, much less Liam, was not what she wanted to do right now. She'd worked her whole life to build up a protective wall around her heart, and there was no need to start breaking that down now.

Unrolling the toilet paper, she ripped a chunk off and dabbed her cheeks. There. She'd had her pity party, and now it was time to move forward. Time to put on her big girl panties and focus on what she needed to do to get out of the wilderness and back to civilization.

"And away from Liam Davenport," she said under her breath.

She combed her fingers through her hair and rubbed her face. Anything to make her feel a bit more put together. She pressed on the faucet and water dripped from it. After her hands were full, she splashed her face. The cold shocked her system and helped ground her.

After waiting a few minutes more, she straightened her clothes and unlatched the bathroom door. As she swung it open, she yelped. Liam was leaning against the wall, inches from her.

He had a look on his face that she couldn't quite read. It was a mixture of amusement and concern. The depth to his gaze and quirked smile made her heart pound in her ears. Dumb emotions. They were going haywire.

"Morning," he said as he pushed off the wall.

"Good morning," she said, mustering a business-like tone. There was no way she wanted to talk about what happened last night, and she hoped that her chilly disposition would hint to that.

He eyed her as she walked past. "Did you sleep well?" There was a playfulness to his voice that caused heat to race to her cheeks.

"Well, I'm in a crashed plane in God knows where. What do you think?" She couldn't let his obvious attempt at flirting derail her. She couldn't let people into her life. They hurt her. They *always* hurt her.

When he didn't return her retort, she glanced over to him. His jaw muscles were flinching as he watched her.

"You're in a bad mood," he said.

She shrugged.

He studied her for a moment before he let out a growl, walked into the bathroom, and slammed the door.

Madeline winced as regret flooded her chest. As she clenched her fists, she took a deep breath. She couldn't feel bad about this. She needed to stay away from Liam. Far away. It was better for her and better for him. He was off-limits. The sooner she accepted that, the better. Even if her heart twisted at the thought. Her head won over. Liam Davenport was off-limits.

LIAM

After a few splashes of cold water to his face, Liam's anger simmered. What had he done? It wasn't like he begged Madeline to crawl into bed with him. She'd done that herself.

He shook his head. What had that been last night? The fear that surrounded her had been almost tangible. There was something in her past that had her spooked. It wasn't just the plane crash—even though she seemed desperate to convince him that it was. There was something more to it. A deep-rooted fear.

As much as he wanted to hate her for how she'd treated him, he couldn't. Perhaps she was as broken as he was, and he couldn't fault her for that. After all, if he wasn't his father then she wasn't her past.

He scrubbed his face as he studied his reflection. His heart pounded as he thought about how good it felt to have Madeline wrapped in his arms. She fit against him. The warmth of her body and feeling of her skin under his hands seemed burned into his mind.

Focus, Liam, he chanted in his mind. They needed to get out of the mountains today and below the snow line before it got dark. Then, they needed to find shelter. He didn't have time to act like a teenage boy.

He opened the bathroom door and walked out. Madeline was sitting on a nearby chair with her knees pulled up, eating crackers. She glanced over to him and then dropped her gaze.

Liam contemplated telling her just what he thought of her sudden chilly disposition but decided against it. He wasn't going to stoop to her level. He'd rise above.

"Are you ready for today?"

She had just shoved a cracker in her mouth, so she nodded.

"Good." He eyed her footwear. Stiletto heels weren't really hiking shoes. "Are those all you have?" he asked as he nodded toward her feet.

She followed his gesture with her gaze. "Yes," she whispered.

Liam scoffed. "Those aren't going to work." He paused.

"Maybe . . ." He made his way to the back of the plane and pulled open a closet. "Yes!" he exclaimed as he pulled a pair of ski boots from inside. Then he walked back over. "Here. Put these on."

She eyed them. "What are these?"

"You don't know what ski boots are?"

"No."

"They're designed to help hold skis to your feet."

She pulled them toward her and slipped off her heels. Liam turned and rifled around in his duffel bag.

"Here're some socks," he said as he handed them to her. Once the boots were secured, she stood.

"Anything else?" she asked.

Liam began packing the backpack he'd found in the closet. He made his way over to her suitcase and rifled around in it again. He wanted to make sure he didn't miss anything. They needed all the supplies they could find. "Just making sure everything's ready to go."

His cheeks heated as he pulled out a few pairs of her undergarments and shoved them into the backpack. Then he shut it and pushed her suitcase to the side.

"Wait. We're not taking that with us?" she asked, her voicing rising an octave as she walked over to the luggage and pulled it toward her.

Liam braced himself for the inevitable fight. "We can't take that with us, Ms. Abernathy. I'm not sure where we are or how far we need to go to get off this mountain. It will only slow us down."

"But—"

He stepped toward her. He needed to get her to understand. "This isn't personal. I'm not trying to hurt you." He was inches from her, and he felt her tense as he stepped closer.

For a moment, he allowed a smile. He was enjoying the ability he had to evoke emotions from her. He leaned in and allowed the feeling of her petite frame inches away from him rush over his body.

Plus, it didn't hurt that she looked so dang cute in his clothes.

Warning bells went off in his mind, so he cleared his throat and backed away. He was getting too close. He needed some distance from her. "It's just not possible for us bring it with." Had he said that before? He couldn't remember. All his brain focused on right now was how beautiful the small splash of freckles was that ran across her nose.

She chewed her bottom lip and then sighed. "Fine. But, you're a billionaire. If you come back for your stuff, I expect you to grab mine as well."

Liam shot out his hand. "Deal."

She eyed it and then returned his gesture. He tried to ignore how soft her skin felt against his. He backed up and made his way over to the closet. He shoved some things around.

He breathed a sigh of relief. The ski boots weren't the only thing still there. All his ski equipment he'd taken on his trip a week ago was still inside. He grabbed the jacket.

"Here," he said, walking over to Madeline.

She slipped it on. It hung off of her like a potato sack. He smiled.

"What?" she asked as she raised and lowered her arms a few times.

"Nothing."

Then, he pulled out everything he could find to keep them warm. Hats, gloves, scarves were soon dumped onto the couch.

"Grab some," he said, waving toward the pile.

Madeline stood and made her way over. She picked a few and returned to her spot.

Desperate for a distraction, Liam took the remaining pairs and shoved them into the backpack. Next, he grabbed a tarp that was stashed in the back and shook out the material. He then spread it open on the ground. He'd make a makeshift pack with it.

He grabbed extra clothes, a pot and utensils from the kitchen, and the first aid kit. After gathering a few more provisions, he laid them in the middle of the tarp.

He peered over at Madeline, who was watching him. She had on an expression that he couldn't quite read. Why was she such a mystery to him? And why did he care?

He made his way to the kitchen and grabbed the remaining cans of food. It wasn't much, but it would work for a meal tonight. They couldn't store too much with the bears that roamed Alaska.

He put the food in the backpack and wrapped the tarp around the rest of the provisions. He folded it into a square and then grabbed some rope that he'd packed in his duffel bag.

"What are you doing?" Madeline asked.

He glanced over to her. "It's called a Yukon pack. I can pack out more stuff doing it this way than that tiny backpack."

Her gaze landed on the backpack. "Is that what I'm carrying?"

Liam nodded. "Yep."

Madeline walked over and grabbed it. Then, she made her way over to her suitcase and rifled around in it. After taking out a few items, she shoved them into the backpack. Liam tried not to notice that one of those items included the picture of her boyfriend.

"What's his name?" he asked, hoping it didn't sound like he cared as much as he seemed to. Man, what was wrong with him?

"Brett."

"Huh. How long have you two been dating?"

When she fell silent, he peeked over at her. She was staring at her hands.

"Three years."

His eyes widened. They must be serious. "Three years? Wow. Are you two going to get hitched?" For some, unknown reason, he held his breath.

"Maybe." Her voice was quiet as if she were trying to hide something.

Liam just brushed it off. It must have been his desire for her to be unsure, that's what it was. His weird, messed-up desire for her to be single.

His stomach growled, so he made his way over to the kitchen and grabbed a box of crackers. In the wilderness, it was better to bring things that couldn't get wet. All the boxed items were going to be left behind.

He ripped open the box and shook it out into a bowl. He whistled over to Duke who'd been sleeping all morning. He stood and shook his body, sending his hair flying in a hairy cloud.

Madeline's nose wrinkled as she moved away from him. Wow. She was pretentious. It took a special kind of person to hate Duke. Everyone loved him. He was the best friend that Liam could ever ask for. It bugged him that Madeline didn't like Duke.

"Eat," he commanded, and Duke happily shoved his nose into the bowl.

When he got the second box down, he ripped it open and started eating. Making his way over to the chair, he settled down on it and watched as Madeline returned to filling the backpack with her items.

"You're going to want to be careful," he said.

She glanced over to him. "About what?"

"You don't want you pack to get too heavy. Who knows the terrain we're going to have to get through until we reach civilization." He grabbed another handful of crackers and shoved them into his mouth.

She fiddled with the clasp of the bag. "Okay." Then she grabbed her purse and started to remove items from it. Her wallet and sunglasses—a book.

Liam debated about telling her not to take it but then stopped himself. Sometimes, experience was the best teacher. Besides, they could always use it to stoke a fire. Which reminded him . . .

"Do you have any tampons?" he asked.

Her cheeks reddened as she turned. "Excuse me?"

He stared at her. Why was this such an embarrassing thing? He knew women menstruated. At least, his fifth-grade teachers made sure that he knew no matter how traumatizing it was to a young kid.

"Tampons. Do you have any?"

Her eyes widened. "Is Aunt Flow visiting you right now?"

He stared at her. "Aunt what? No, it's for starting fires. Who's Aunt Flow?" Then he stopped. Aunt Flow. Menstruation. He put the pieces together. "Never mind."

She widened her eyes as she nodded. Then, she shoved her hand into her purse and emerged with a few.

"Perfect. Make sure to pack those. Oh, and if you have any pads, throw them in as well."

He stood and brushed off the crumbs that had accumulated on his pant legs.

Duke finished his crackers and stood, whimpering at the door.

"I'm coming, buddy," Liam called out as he made his way over and pushed the door open.

Duke disappeared into the powdery snow.

Liam glanced at his watch. It was seven in the morning. They needed to get moving if they were going to get anywhere before nightfall. During the fall in Alaska, the sun set six minutes earlier every day. They couldn't afford to get stuck without shelter when the sun went down.

"Ready to go?" he called over to her. He shoved his feet into this boots and laced them up.

Madeline pulled on her hat and gloves. Liam helped her with the backpack that seemed to want to get caught on the baggy parts of the jacket.

Then, he secured the Yukon pack and waved for Madeline to help him up. Once standing, he grabbed the remaining water bottles and shoved them into his coat pocket. No use letting them go to waste.

Liam glanced around the airplane and a sense of sadness

washed over him. This was his baby. The only link he had to his father. And he was deserting it in the wilderness.

He reached out and pressed his hand on one of the walls. "I'll come find you," he whispered.

He made his way to the cockpit and grabbed the map, compass, and flare gun that he kept there. Once they get out of the mountains, he'd plot a path west—toward the ocean. Hopefully, they'd run into a hunting pack or signal a plane and this entire nightmare would be over with.

Just before he left, he paused. Walking over to the closet, he pulled out his rifle and bear spray. Hopefully, he wouldn't have to use either, but it was better to be prepared than not. He also reached in and grabbed his two ski poles. They would be helpful in trying to navigate the uneven terrain.

When he passed by Madeline, her eyes widened as she nodded to the gun and spray. "Are we going to need those?"

He glanced at her. "Hopefully not. But it's better to have them and not need them than need them and not have them." He stopped at the opening and handed her a ski pole. "Are you ready, Ms. Abernathy?"

Madeline chewed her lip as she glanced outside. "Don't really have a choice now, do I?"

Liam smiled. "It'll be fun. After all, what's the worst that could happen?"

CHAPTER NINE

MADELINE

*M*adeline pulled her coat tighter around her body as she stood on the mountain, waiting for Liam to join her. Duke was barking and throwing his head around in powdery snow. She shook her head. This should be interesting. Trying to survive with a hyper, four-legged creature.

She glanced around, and her heart pounded. Huge mountains rose up on either side of them. As she took in the white tips, she felt thankful they hadn't crashed up so high. She could only imagine what it would be like to try to get down from up there.

She turned her attention back to the stretch of rocks and snow that spanned out in front of them. The sun was hidden by the clouds, but occasionally, it would peek through, basking the ground with its light.

Liam's jumped from the doorway. A look of sadness washed over his expression. She eyed the grounded plane. He seemed to have this attachment to the hunk of metal. For a moment, she wondered what that was.

He straightened his Yukon pack and glanced around until his

gaze landed on her. As if sensing her questions, he waved back to the plane. "It was a gift." His voice dropped an octave. "From my father."

Madeline's eyes widened. What must that be like? Getting a plane for one's birthday?

Liam shook his head. "It's not like that."

"It was a plane," Madeline breathed out.

Liam glanced around and then motioned for her to follow him. They started walking through the snow. It wasn't as easy as it looked. Occasional rocks jutted up from underneath the snow and ski boots weren't padded. Madeline tried not to wince as her foot shifted against the hard plastic.

"You have to stop thinking about things in terms of dollar amounts. Instead, it's all about ratios," Liam said, falling into step with her.

"What does that mean?"

"How much did you parents make when you were kid?"

At the mention of her parents, Madeline's twisted her neck to loosen the tension. It didn't help that she'd slept somewhat elevated with her head kinked. "Eighty thousand."

Liam nodded as he studied the snow in front of him. "And what was your favorite Christmas present?"

"You mean, besides the ones that Santa got me?" This conversation was making her uncomfortable. The truth was her parents weren't extremely concerned with making a little girl's Christmas dreams come true. She was lucky if she got a present at all.

Liam shot her a look. "Come on."

She steeled her expression. "Sorry. Um . . ." Lie. It was always better to lie then have uncomfortable conversations about her past. "A doll."

Liam squinted. "And they cost, what? A hundred?"

Madeline stopped. "A hundred dollars? Where do you buy your dolls?"

Liam's cheeks heated. "I've never bought a doll."

Madeline stuck her ski pole out to steady herself as she continued moving down the mountain. "I'm not surprised."

"Okay, so, what, twenty?" he said, as he walked behind her.

"Yeah. That's probably about right."

"If your father made eighty thousand a year and he bought you a doll for Christmas, that's . . ." He grew silent. She peeked behind her to see that his jaw was set, and he was studying the snow as they walked. "That means you father spent, .025 percent on your present."

Madeline turned around. That was impressive. "You came up with that in your head?"

Liam didn't meet her gaze. "Just cause I'm rich, doesn't mean I'm dumb."

Her eyes widened. "I never said that rich people were dumb."

His glanced at her. "I did not get that from how you've been treating me."

"Me? Treating you? What about the way you've been treating me?"

His Adam's apple rose and fell as he studied her. "How have I been treating you?" He turned and whistled to Duke who was wandering away. The dog turn, perked up his ears, and then raced back over.

Her throat tightened. It was as if her body was trying to keep her feelings inside. History had taught her that expressing your thoughts got you hurt. It gave another ammunition to use against you. And she wasn't sure she was ready to give Liam that kind of power over her.

"Just forget about it," she said as she moved ahead. The snow puffed up around her feet as she stomped through it. The clouds had parted, and the sun was beating down on her. It felt good. It helped warm up her chilled skin.

"I'm sorry." Liam's voice made her jump. She should have heard the crunching of the snow as he made his way to her, but she was too muddled up in her mind to take notice.

"For what?"

"For whatever it is that I did to upset you."

She turned. "You're apologizing, and you don't know for what?"

His lips tightened. "I'm just being a gentleman."

Heat raced to her cheeks. "Don't do that. Don't just apologize because you think it's the right thing to do. Do it because you feel sorry, or don't do it at all."

He eyed her. "But—"

She shook her head. She hated phonies. People doing things because society told them it was the right thing to do. One of the reasons she wanted to be a journalist was to challenge the norm.

"Okay," he said

She turned and smiled. Perhaps, she could teach Mr. Rich Man a thing or two.

They continued down the mountain in silence. Duke raced around, sniffing and licking at random things. Madeline peered over at Liam. She hated the awkwardness that surrounded them.

"You were talking about percentages?"

He glanced over at her, and his expression was blank for a moment. Then he nodded. "Right, percentages. So, for your gift, your father spent .025 percent of his yearly income. For my father to buy me a plane, it cost .6 of a percent. That's it."

Madeline coughed at that number. "What? Are you serious? It cost your father less than one percent of his income to buy you a private plane?"

"Well, not yearly income—net worth. But, yeah. That's about right."

Madeline gawked at him. She knew he was rich, but this put things in a completely different perspective. "Wow. You . . ." Words didn't form in her mind. How does one comprehend that much money?

Liam shifted his pack as he glanced around. "It's not always all it's cracked up to be, though."

Madeline blew into her gloves, trying to warm up her fingers. "How is that even possible? Literally everything you want can be bought. Everything."

His gaze found its way back to hers. "Not everything."

There was a sadness in his expression. A longing for something that she couldn't quite pick out. A surge raced through her. Perhaps he knew what it was like to be abandoned just as she did. She parted her lips to say something—anything—to help him feel better, but nothing came. Instead, she pressed her lips together and nodded.

They stood in silence for a moment before Liam waved his hand. "We should keep moving," he said.

Madeline nodded and followed after him. As she watched his pack shift as he walked, her thoughts raced around in her mind. Was it possible that this billionaire could relate to her? Here he was getting a plane for his birthday, but deep down, all he wanted was to be loved and accepted?

She shook her head as she wrapped her thumbs around the straps of her backpack. Having these thoughts about Liam wasn't going to help her keep a journalistic mind about him. They were going to stilt her opinions, and then she wouldn't be able to write an unbiased article.

She chewed her cheek as she sighed. Being a journalist was all she had left, and she couldn't throw it away on sympathy for Liam Davenport. She needed to keep him at arm's length if she was going to survive in the wilderness and her heart.

LIAM

Darkness crept around them as they continued their descent down of the mountain. Liam glanced at his watch. That was strange. They'd been hiking for a few hours, yet it felt as if evening was approaching. He glanced up to the sky and anxiety raced through his nerves as he saw the cloud that was inching closer. A storm was coming.

Panic pricked the back of his neck as he kept his gaze on the distance below. He squinted to see better, and a flood of relief raced through him. It was a glacier. And just like rivers, glaciers ran downstream. If they followed it, they just might be able to get off the mountain before nightfall.

Liam paused. There was a good three-hundred-foot decline down the mountain from where they stood until they reached the glacier. With the darkness of the clouds rolling in, he knew they didn't have the time to hike down it. They needed to get off the face of the mountain and fast.

He grabbed his ski pole and bent it around his knee. There was only one way of getting down in a timely manner.

"What's wrong?" Madeline asked as she came up from behind him.

He bent the pole in the opposite direction until the metal became pliable and snapped. "We needed to slide down the mountain."

When she didn't reply, he glanced over at her.

"I'm sorry, what?" Her face paled as she peered down the mountain face.

"We need to slide down."

"Like, a slide-slide."

He nodded. "We're going to use this as an anchor to help control our speed."

Madeline shook her head. "Nope. Not doing that. I can't do that." Her eyes were wide as she glanced around. "Six-hundred thousand people are injured while skiing every year." She paused. "Six-hundred thousand," she said, dragging out each syllable.

"Madeline, listen. You're going to be fine. I'm going down with you." He walked over to her backpack and unzipped it. He pulled out the extra rope he'd stashed inside.

"We're going down together?" She turned. Her eyes were wide.

He nodded.

She eyed him and then eyed the mountain. "How do I know that you're not going to use me as sled?"

His lips twitched as that image passed through his mind. "Well . . ."

She smacked his arm. "Hey!"

He shielded himself with his hand. "Don't hit the person who holds your future in their hands."

She narrowed her eyes. "Is this really the only way?"

He tied the rope around his waist and motioned toward the clouds that were rolling in at a rapid pace. "See those? You don't want to be stuck in the storm they're bringing in. We need to get off of this mountain and fast."

Madeline turned and stared where he was motioning. "Do you think we can beat it?"

Liam nodded. "If you trust me."

She pursed her lips and then turned back. "Okay."

He paused. "Really?"

She nodded. "I trust you enough to do this."

A spark of pride raced through his chest. Madeline actually trusted him to do something. It was the first time in a long time that he felt the pressure of expectation bearing down on him, and yet he wanted nothing more than to prove that he could do it.

He stepped forward until he was inches away from her. Her body tensed as he moved his arms on both sides of her waist and threaded the rope around her.

He could feel her body next to his as he drew closer so the distance between the rope was only about a foot. He needed to keep her closely tethered to him.

"Liam?" her voice was barely a whisper.

He leaned back to look into her eyes. They were a dark green. He could feel her fear emanating off of her. "Yes?"

"Are you scared?"

Their previous conversation raced through his mind. He

wanted to admit that he was. But, she needed him to be strong, so he would be. He gave her a smile, which caused her to roll her eyes. "Of course not. This is easy. Simple stuff." He tightened the knot he had just tied with a bit more gusto than needed. Then he grabbed their bags and pushed them down the mountain. They disappeared under the encroaching cloud.

She turned to look at him and then sighed. "If you're confident, then I'm confident."

He nodded. "All right, lie down."

They had to move together until they were lying side by side. Liam dug his foot into the snow to keep himself from slipping down. Madeline seemed to be doing the same thing.

He moved the bent ski pole around in the snow until he got it deep enough. Inside, he was praying that he'd be able to control their descent. There were two things that could happen. One, what he planned. He'd use the pole to keep them from slipping too fast down the mountain and they'd stop at the bottom. Or two, he would lose control. The pole would be ripped from his hands, and they'd go tumbling down.

He tightened his jaw as he focused on the first one. It wasn't only his life that depended on him being successful, but Madeline's as well. He'd be successful. He had to.

"Ready?" he asked as he glanced over to her. Her face was white as the snow around them.

"I think so," she squeaked out.

Liam looked up to Duke. Thankfully, being a mountain dog had its perks. "Come find us, buddy, when you get down," he said.

Duke barked as he paced through the snow. Hopefully, as they started heading down the mountain, Duke would follow after them. Liam wished he could do something more to help, but there was no way he could get down with the two of them tied to him.

He took a deep breath and blew it out. It was now or never. The storm was rolling in faster than he could think. They needed to get down, and now.

"Let's go," Liam said.

Madeline scooted closer to him and wrapped her arms around his middle. She tucked her face against his chest and nodded into it.

Liam closed his eyes for a moment as he gathered his courage and then pushed off with his hands. After a few good shoves, they started down the mountain.

CHAPTER TEN

MADELINE

*M*adeline's body ached as they raced down the mountainside. She tucked in closer to Liam as the wind whipped around her. The air was so cold that it stung her skin. She kept her eyes pinched shut and her lips pulled taut.

She winced as a rock slammed into her side. She heard a moan rattle Liam's chest. He twitched as if he were trying to fight the urge to release everything he was holding on to. The rock must have hit him differently than her.

It felt like an eternity until the pitch was no longer as steep, and they began to slow. Once they came to a stop, Madeline lay there, not wanting to move. There was a strength to Liam that sucked her in, and she didn't want to let go.

He groaned again as he tried to move. Suddenly, she realized she might be hurting him. Or annoying him. She pulled back as far as the rope would allow her to and glanced over at him.

His eyes were pinched shut, and his face was contorted into a look of pain. He was hurt. Her heart raced as she ran her gaze up and down his body. There was no blood that she could see.

"Liam?" she asked, scooting closer to him and peering into his face.

He moaned again.

"Are you hurt? Where does it hurt?" She glanced down at his body again. What was wrong?

"My—ribs," he breathed out as he shifted to pull up his jacket.

"Your ribs?" Madeline repeated as she sat up and helped him with his shirt. She sucked in her breath when she saw the red and blue bruise that crept across his right rib cage.

She reached out and gently touched them.

He winced.

"Sorry," she whispered.

He kept his head back as his eyes squeezed shut. "It's okay."

"You got this from just now?" She studied the bruise. It didn't look fresh. Like it'd been there for a day.

He shook his head. "I bruised them during the landing yesterday. But that rock didn't help." He opened his eyes and kept his gaze toward the sky.

"You had this yesterday?"

Liam nodded.

"Why didn't you tell me?"

He peered over at her as he winced and pulled himself up to lean back on his elbow. "You didn't ask."

She scoffed. "As much as we don't like it, we're a team out here. We need to be honest with each other. And tell each other when we've been injured."

Liam studied her as his jaw tightened and then relaxed. "Okay."

"Really?"

He shrugged. "Sure." Then he paused. "You annoy me." He pushed some snow around with his gloved hand.

She stared at him. "What?"

"You said to be honest, so I'm being honest. You annoy me."

Madeline let out an exasperated sigh. "I annoy you?" How

could he say that? Especially when it was so obvious that he was the annoying one in this relationship.

He nodded as he winced and straightened. Then he started untying the rope.

Once she was free, she stood and paced a few feet away from him. His words racing through her like a hot liquid she'd just swallowed.

"Madeline." Liam's voice broke through her thoughts. She turned to see him smiling at her.

"What?"

"Stop taking things so seriously," he said as he winced again. He'd turned to put his hands underneath him, but then he paused.

"What?" she asked again.

He glanced over at her. "It's a joke. I'm just teasing you. You take life a bit too seriously."

She folded her arms. "I take it too seriously? What about you? Don't you take anything seriously?"

He stopped trying to stand and, instead, rested his arms on his raised knees. "What does that mean?"

She shrugged as she walked back and forth. They were on top of the glacier now. The snow crunched under her feet. It spanned out in either direction for as far as she could see.

"Why didn't you go to your father's funeral?" she asked, the words tumbled from her lips.

His expression steeled as he glanced at her. Madeline knew she'd struck a nerve, but Liam shouldn't dish it out if he couldn't take it.

He pushed a rock against the snow. "It's complicated."

That was a ridiculous excuse. She wasn't going to let him get away with that. "How complicated can it be? You show up in a suit and pay your respects. Doesn't seem that complicated." She should know. Plus, she'd been just a kid when she had to do it with her parents. He was a grown man. He should have been stronger.

His gaze turned icy. "What do you know? Have you buried a parent?"

Madeline's heart squeezed in her chest. Watching both caskets get lowered into the ground was one of the worst experiences of her life. Even to this day, when that memory haunted her, tears would form on her lids. Stupid emotions.

Not wanting Liam to see her cry, she turned and stared off into the distance. From behind her, she heard him swear under his breath. It was followed by the sound of him shifting to stand.

She wiped at the tears that escaped. Why was she so weak? She should be strong. That's how you got through life. Never letting people hurt you. Ever.

"I'm sorry," he said as he approached her.

Madeline wrapped her arms around her chest and nodded. It wasn't his fault that she had a messed-up past. He didn't know. She couldn't fault him for that. It just really bothered her that he didn't even try to show up to his dad's funeral. After all, he did buy Liam a plane. That showed that Richard Davenport had at least been an interested father. That was more than she could say about her own parents.

He stood next to her in silence. She let the tears flow for a few minutes more before she took a deep breath. That was the allotted time she'd give herself to cry over her parents, and then, she'd wipe them away and move on.

"Was it your mom?" he asked as he peered over at her.

Her body felt heavy as the headstone for her parents floated through her mind. "And my dad."

"I'm sorry," he said again. He reached out and wrapped his arm around her shoulders.

There was something about standing on a giant frozen river with Liam's arm wrapped around her that calmed her nerves. There was an understanding that was felt. It didn't need to be vocalized.

A barking in the distance drew her attention behind her.

Glancing back, she saw Duke bounding across the snow toward them.

Liam dropped his arm and clapped his hands. "You found us, buddy!" he exclaimed. He bent down and reached out to grab the dog.

But instead of running into his owner's arms, Duke raced up to Madeline and practically leaped into her arms. She screamed and shielded her face, anticipating the bite that was sure to come.

The weight of his body threw her backward, and she landed hard on her butt. Her breath left her body as he pinned her to the ground. He shoved his face into hers and started licking.

"Liam!" she shrieked as she wiggled to get out from under Duke.

Liam laughed. "What? He loves you. Didn't you see how he ran for you instead of me?"

"Get him off," she pleaded. Duke didn't relent with his kisses.

Liam's soft chuckle grew louder as he neared. "You heard her, bud. Get off."

Duke glanced over to Liam. Finally, it took Liam grabbing his collar and pulling to get the animal off her. She lay on the ice, staring up at the sky. What a strange experience this was. Stranded with a billionaire and his overly loving canine. She exhaled, shielded her eyes, and glanced over to Liam.

He was studying the landscape that spanned out in front of them. His eyes were squinted as if he were trying to figure out the distance.

"What?" she asked, sitting up and wrapping her arms around her knees.

"Just trying to estimate how far away we are. I hope we can get out of the snow line before dark."

Madeline's heart picked up speed as she took in Liam's tone. She didn't know a lot about Alaska, but she did know they had bears and freezing temperatures. Neither of which she wanted to be introduced to.

She stood and glanced over to him. "Well, let's get going."

Liam nodded and walked over to where his pack had landed and put it on. Madeline found hers and shouldered it as well.

Once they were situated, Liam nodded in the direction that he wanted them to go, and she followed after him. She had so many questions racing through her mind, but she bit her lip to keep them there. What happened at the funeral? He hadn't really answered the question. Where was his mom? Why did he get all clammed up when she mentioned his family? And last but not least, the most exposing question of all: why did her heart beat faster when he touched her?

LIAM

They had to reach the end of the glacier soon. They just had to. They'd been walking for a few hours now, and yet, there was nothing but snow and mountain in front of them. The only saving grace he could find was that the crevices in the glacier were slowly getting wider, which meant the end was a bit closer.

He heard a struggle and then Madeline's exasperated sigh. He glanced behind him and saw that she'd slipped. Again.

"Can we just stop a second?" she asked as she lay back on the ice.

"No," he said, motioning for her to get up.

"But—" she started as she moved to stand only to have her feet go out from underneath her again. She groaned and shot him an angry look. "You have boots. I have this ski-nonsense footwear." She waved her hand toward his ski boots and sighed.

"I know. Once we're out of the snow and ice, you can take them off."

She bit her lip as she brought her elbow up and leaned back on it. "How much longer?"

He peered out in front of them. "Soon."

She groaned as she turned to her hands and knees and pushed

back. He reached out and grabbed her elbow. He tried to ignore the surge of electricity that shot up his hand from her touch. It rattled him in a way that touching a woman had never done before.

Once she was stable, he pulled his hand away and wiped it on his jeans. For his health, he needed to stop touching Madeline Abernathy. With the current that rushed through his body mixed with these plummeting temperatures, he was sure to have a heart attack.

"Come on, you can rest once we're on the ground." He glanced over at her and couldn't help but notice that her cheeks were flushed. There was a look in her eye that told him she'd felt the connection too.

She nodded as she followed after him.

As the crevices grew larger, he led her over to the edge where the mountain met the glacier. Here, the rocks would make the path a little harder to walk on, but at least they wouldn't be in danger of falling in through one of the crevices and disappearing into the depths of the glacier.

He let Madeline take the lead. The boots made it difficult for her to find her footing, and he wanted to be behind her to help her if she slipped. Which had started happening—more and more.

After another half hour of walking on the rocks, Madeline slipped and this time she stayed down.

"Liam, I can't. I just can't." She pulled up her feet and started unbuckling the ski boots.

Liam knelt down next to her and helped her slide them off. He cradled her heel in his hand as he pulled the liner and her sock off. He sucked in his breath as he took in her raw skin.

"Why didn't you tell me?" he asked, pulling off his pack and untying it so he could get out the first aid kit. He grabbed a bottle of water so he could dab her foot.

"I didn't want you to think I was weak," she whispered.

He glanced up at her, and his heart surged. She looked so fragile. So desperately in need of something, that every part of his being wanted to give it to her. If only he could figure out what that was.

"I don't think you're weak," he said as he grabbed the ointment and dabbed it on her blisters.

She was silent, so he glanced up at her. Her brows were furrowed as she studied him.

"You don't know me. We've been crashed for, what, a day?" She sighed as she grabbed the bottle of water that he'd set down and drank from it.

"So tell me something about you. Something that you've never told anyone." He grabbed a bandage and ripped open the packaging.

She was silent again. He continued to work, trying to allow her some time to think.

She shifted against the snow. "Okay, here's one. I'm terrified about going to the bathroom out in the wilderness."

Liam chuckled as he glanced up at her. "Not the outdoor type of person?" he asked as he removed the other ski boot and started working on cleaning up her cuts.

"Nah. Never really got into it."

He nodded. "Well, that one doesn't count. Everyone is scared of using the bathroom in the woods. Tell me something else."

She sighed. "Okay. Hmm. Here's one. My roommate has a total crush on you. She'd probably have a heart attack if she knew I was stranded in the Alaskan wilderness getting first aid from you."

The corner of his lips tipped up into a half smile. "She has a crush on me?"

Madeline reached out and swatted his arm. "Don't look ᴄ pleased. She had a crush on Captain Crunch when we were ᴵ

"From the cereal?"

"Yes. See, she's not hard to please."

Liam chuckled as he applied another bandaℊ

grew quiet. "Captain Crunch. Well, at least she has good taste. It is the best breakfast cereal."

"Yeah. She said her psychic told her you two were meant to be together."

"Oh, really?" He was starting to like this roommate of hers. She seemed like quite a character.

Madeline nodded. "Just a heads-up."

He slipped the boot insert back onto her foot. "Well, I'll keep that in mind." He smiled at her, and she returned it. He was really starting to like it when she smiled.

Once the boot was secured, he reached out his hand and she grabbed onto it. He pulled her up. She winced as she put pressure on her feet. She took a step forward, but her legs buckled, and Liam reached out to grab her before she fell.

She felt so good in his arms that it took all his strength not to pull her closer. He was lying to himself if he said he didn't enjoy how she'd started to loosen up around him. There was a mystery to Madeline that he wanted to solve—that he was desperate to solve.

"I promise, as soon as we get out of the mountains, you can take those off," he whispered in her ear.

For a moment, he thought he felt her shiver. If that were true, it was most likely from the cold weather and not the closeness of their bodies.

"Okay," she whispered as she pushed off his chest.

Reluctantly, he let her go.

Madeline paused as she glanced up at him. "We should get going."

Liam nodded, letting her lead the way. As he followed behind her, he cursed his pounding heart. There was no way he could allow himself to feel anything but platonic toward Ms. Abernathy. Even if he forgot how to do the simplest tasks when he was around her.

CHAPTER ELEVEN

MADELINE

*M*adeline shivered again as she walked alongside the mountain. The memory of Liam's body pressed against her raced through her mind. She shook her head hard. It needed to leave. Now.

Before she slipped into madness from trying to decipher Liam's intentions, she stopped. In the distance, she could see trees and greenery. She turned.

"Look!" She pointed to the change in landscape.

A smile spread across Liam's lips. "Finally. The end of the glacier."

Seeing the first sign of life had healing effects on Madeline. Suddenly, the pinching and throbbing sensation in her feet lessened. She was almost out of this mountain. Freedom was just moments away.

As they neared the edge of the glacier, the joy in Madeline's heart plummeted. There was a good hundred-foot drop into a lake in front of them. Streams ran from the glacier and down the front of the mountain. How the heck were they going to get down?

"Liam?" she asked as she turned to look at him. "What now?"

Liam's posture had tightened as he looked around. He glanced at Madeline and then over to Duke. He peered over the edge and pushed his hands through his hair. When his gaze met hers, a tingle erupted in her stomach. He was worried. Mr. Mountaineer Man was worried. This wasn't good.

"Liam? What's wrong?"

He grabbed his bag and opened it. "I—" He looked behind him again. "I just don't think I can lower you with the rope."

Madeline tapped her temples. "What? Lower me down?"

He'd pulled out the rope they'd used earlier. "There are two options we have. The first—I lower you and Duke down and then you lower me down. The second—we go through the glacier and hope we pick the tunnel that takes us out."

She glanced over to the glacier. "How likely are we to pick the wrong one?"

Liam's Adam's apple rose and fell as he fiddled with the rope. "Probably fifty-fifty. If we pick the wrong one, we will disappear into the glacier and never come out."

Madeline's legs weakened. What did he just say? "Disappear into the glacier? Um, let's try the waterfall." She walked closer to the edge, but seeing the drop up close didn't make her feel any better.

"Madeline, I don't think that's going to work. I think our best bet is to go down one of the tunnels."

"Tunnels? Disappearing into an ice coffin sounds better?"

"Better than falling down a hundred-foot cliff onto jagged rocks."

Madeline's stomach hardened as she thought about what he'd said. All she wanted was to be home right now. Not stuck in the Alaskan wilderness. Why did she come again?

She glanced over at Liam who was studying her.

"Don't say it," he said as he shoved the rope back into his pack and tied it up.

"Say what?"

"The thought that's floating around in your mind." He secured his pack and stood.

"What? The fact that this situation is completely your fault?"

He started toward one of the openings in the glacier. It was about three feet in diameter, and he had to duck to get in it. "Yep. That one." His voice echoed off the walls of the glacier as he disappeared into it.

"Wait," Madeline called after him. She wrapped her thumbs around her backpack straps and moved to the opening.

Liam was sitting down on the bluest ice she'd ever seen. He was tapping it with the ski pole half. She stood a few feet off and waited.

"I understand that I failed. I was the pilot. It was my job to keep you safe." He glanced up, and her breath caught in her throat. There was so much pain in his gaze that she dropped her focus to the ground. The feelings that he stirred in her startled and alarmed her.

An arm reached out causing her to jump. He had appeared in the entrance of the tunnel, and his hand was extended and now cradling her elbow. She brought her gaze up to meet his.

"I will make sure you survive, Ms. Abernathy. I will protect you." His voice deepened with each word. "You just need to trust me."

She stared at him, and her heart surged. Suddenly, he wasn't the billionaire bad boy she'd built up in her mind. He was Liam. A broken and worried man. And she could connect with that.

"Okay," she whispered as she nodded. "I trust you."

Liam eyed her one more time and then dropped his hand. "The ice seems solid, which is a good sign. All we need to do is climb down." He waved toward the tunnels. "It will get claustrophobic in there, but you just have to keep moving."

Madeline eyed the opening. "You're coming down with me. Right?"

Liam nodded. "I'll be right behind you. I need to help Duke down."

She studied the ice. It didn't make her feel comfortable that she had to go first. But, if going second meant she needed to keep Duke safe, she'd rather go first.

"Hey," he said as he stood and brushed her arm with his fingertips. "You can do this."

Madeline nodded but, inside, her heart pounded. Could she do this? She wasn't strong. She couldn't even save her mother from her abusive father. How was she going to make it out of the wilderness? Liam seemed so confident about everything, and she only slowed his pace.

She sat down as she peered into the tunnel. The blue ice glowed from the sunlight. Water seeped into her pants. She flexed her fingers as the coolness of the ice settled into her bones. It was now or never. She took a deep breath and pushed off, slipping into the tunnel. She stifled the scream inside of her throat. It was too late to panic now.

LIAM

Liam watched Madeline disappear into the tunnel. His head pounded as fear rushed through him. What if something happened to her? He used to be so confident in his ability to survive, but now that confidence was gone. Perhaps it had something to do with the fact that two other lives depended on him. When he was alone, it didn't matter if he put himself in life-threatening situations. It was only him.

"Come on, Duke!" he called and then whistled.

Duke poked his head up from behind a mound of rocks. He glanced over to Liam, barked, and then ran over. Liam grabbed hold of his collar and pulled him into the tunnel.

Duke's nails scratched against the ice, but Liam didn't relent. They just needed to get far enough down the tunnel that this entrance was no longer visible. Then Duke would settle down.

"How're you doing, Madeline?" Liam called out. He waited as silence crept around him. He strained to hear her against the sound of his pounding heart.

"It's wet, and my feet hurt." Her voice echoed off the tunnel walls.

He let out the breath he'd been holding. She was safe. "Are you hurt?"

"No."

"Wait where you are. Duke and I will catch up."

"Okay."

Liam dragged Duke down the tunnel, leaning back and leading with his feet. His shoes slipped a few times on the wet ice, but he managed to keep from falling. After a few turns, he found Madeline leaning against a piece of ice that jutted out from the side of the tunnel.

With the entrance now behind them, Duke settled. He lowered his body to the ice and shuffled behind Liam.

"Had to bring the dog," she huffed.

"Duke's my man," Liam said, reaching out and ruffling the dog's hair.

Madeline shook her head.

"You don't like dogs?"

"Is it that obvious?"

Liam eyed her. "How can you not like dogs? It's like a human thing to like them. That's why they're called 'man's best friend.'"

Madeline shifted and slid farther down the tunnel, and Liam followed after her.

"A German shepherd bit me once when I was kid. Ever since then, they haven't been my best friends," she said as she scooted over a hump of ice.

"So, because you had an encounter with one dog that was bad, suddenly all dogs are bad?"

She was quiet for a moment. "It's more about self-preservation. Why allow yourself to trust an animal that might not be trustworthy? Keep yourself at a distance, and they'll never hurt you."

Liam peered down at her. "Are we talking about dogs or people?"

She stopped moving. For a moment, he worried he'd said the wrong thing. She glanced up at him, and his throat tightened. She'd been hurt. And not just from an animal. There were people in her life that had disappointed her. The surge of emotion in his chest told him that he wanted to know what. For some reason, he had a desire to fix the pain that was emanating from her.

He swallowed, willing himself to not speak. He didn't want to scare off this elusive woman. She was intriguing and broken. And every time he spoke to her, he wanted to fix whatever she was struggling with.

He gave her a smile and nodded toward the tunnel. "We should keep going," he said.

She glanced toward where he had motioned and then back over to him. She opened her mouth to say something, but a cracking sound echoed off the walls.

Liam's breath caught in his throat. He didn't have time to think, much less move.

Before he could do anything, a large crack formed between him and Madeline. He let go of Duke's collar and scooted all the way down, reaching out to catch her.

She'd shifted and moved. Her eyes were wide as she reached out to grab his arm. "Help me," she whispered as the ice began to break away from the glacier.

Liam willed his arm to extend farther than he knew it could go. But he came up short. Madeline's fingers eluded his grasp, and the ice chunk she was sitting on broke away, taking her with it. It crashed into the lake below, spraying water around it.

Cursing, Liam studied the drop in front of him. He stared at the chunk of ice, willing Madeline to surface. He was still about sixty feet above the water's surface, but he needed to get down. Now.

She could be trapped under the ice. She could have hit her head on the way down. When she didn't surface, Liam knew he only had moments to get down and save her.

Throwing his pack onto the shore below, he turned onto his stomach and pushed his feet down. He glanced back at Duke.

"Follow me, boy," he said, and then he let go of the edge and plummeted into the icy water. It stung his skin. It felt as if tiny daggers were piercing his body as he broke the surface.

"Madeline!" he called out as he swam toward the ice chunk. He couldn't see her. Taking in a deep breath, he pushed under the water and searched the depths of the lake.

Finally, after what felt like an eternity, he found her sinking a few feet off. Using all the energy he could muster, he swam over to her. Once he had his arm hooked around her, he willed his body toward the surface. But it was so far away. Why was it so far away?

His lungs burned. His heart hammered in his chest. Every part of his body screamed for oxygen. He kicked his legs as he kept pushing to the surface. Eventually he'd get there. Right?

Just before defeat surrounded him, he gave his muscles one last burst, and he broke the water's surface. He gasped for air and tilted back, resting Madeline against his chest. He paused for a moment, sucking in as much air as he could.

When he was no longer gulping the air, he gritted his teeth and made his way toward shore. But, just like the water's surface, the shore seemed so far away. As if he could never get there. Every time he glanced over to the rocky shoreline, his heart sank. It was as if he were crawling toward it.

He rejoiced when he felt the ground under his feet. He half carried, half dragged Madeline onto the shore. After scouting out a flat section of dirt, he forced his muscles to move toward it. After laying her down, he collapsed next to her.

"Madeline?" he asked, his teeth chattering.

Her eyes were closed, and her lips were a pale shade of blue. Cursing, he leaned his ear toward her lips and studied her chest. Nothing.

Prying open her mouth, he covered it with his and blew into her throat. Her ribs rose from the oxygen. He moved to her sternum and pressed down. He counted in his mind each compression, breaking only to breathe more air into her body.

She had to live. She just had to. He'd promised to protect her, and now? She was slipping away from him, and there was nothing he could do.

"Come on, Madeline!" he yelled as he leaned down and filled her lungs with air. His arms had turned numb, but he fought past the pain. He couldn't stop now. "You can't leave me," he whispered as defeat began to settle in around him. If he didn't get his soaked clothes off his body, he wouldn't be able to save himself, much less Madeline. And that wasn't a decision he wanted to make right now.

For all his talk of wanting to be alone, the thought of losing her after he promised to take care of her terrified him. It was the reason he couldn't bring himself to attend his father's funeral. Why he'd been reckless and drunk and crashed his father's boat. The thought of failing yet another person in is life caused his chest to tighten.

"Please," he said as he glanced down at Madeline's pale face. "Don't leave me."

A splash sounded next to him. Glancing over, he saw Duke had jumped into the water from above. As he continued chest compressions, Liam watched as the dog swam toward the shore. He was grateful for the distraction that watching Duke brought.

He couldn't turn his attention back to Madeline's ashen skin and lifeless body. He feared that if he did look, then he would need to acknowledge that she was gone. And that he had failed. Again.

His teeth chattered as he closed his eyes. Thirty more seconds, then he'd stop. He'd give her thirty more seconds before he needed to find warmth for himself. He peered down at her.

"You hear that? Thirty more seconds, then you need to come to or I have to stop." He counted down in his mind. Inside, he pleaded with her to wake up.

A sputtering sound broke his concentration. Glancing down, his heart soared. She was coughing up water, and color was returning to her skin. He helped turn her to her side, and she threw up onto the ground.

When she was finished, he helped her sit up and then threw his arms around her.

"You're alive," he breathed, taking every moment to enjoy the feeling of her body against his. He stretched out his fingers to feel her chest rise and fall.

She shivered as she nodded into his shoulder.

Warmth. She needed warmth. "I'll be right back," he said, suddenly invigorated with the task at hand.

He raced around as fast as he could, grabbing dried branches. The movement helped keep his muscles warm. The thought of Madeline catching hypothermia stoked the fire in his stomach.

He could save her. And he wouldn't stop until he did.

CHAPTER TWELVE

MADELINE

*M*adeline had never felt so cold in her life. Everything shivered as she sat on the shore, watching Liam build a fire.

A fire.

She closed her eyes as she envisioned sitting next to the fire-place at Christmastime. Its warmth surrounding her body.

If only she didn't have to wake up. She was so happy here.

"Madeline. Wake up." Liam's voice cut through her reverie.

She moaned and pinched her eyes shut. Why was he taking her away from this memory? It was too welcoming. Here, her body was relaxed, and her mind was calm.

"Wake up!"

A hard shake to her shoulder snapped her from the dream she wished was a reality. Opening her eyes, she glanced up. Liam had unpacked his pack and had shaken out a sleeping bag next to her.

He was unbuttoning his shirt as he studied her.

"Wh-wh-what a-are you d-d-doing?" she asked, shivers cutting up each word.

"Your body is going into shock from the cold. We need to warm you up." He stripped off his shirt and laid it by the fire.

Fire.

The yellow and orange flames licked the wood. It looked warm, but Madeline couldn't feel any of it. Part of her wanted to climb into it. To feel something on her numb skin.

"Th-that was f-f-fast."

"You're lucky that I won fastest fire maker in Boy Scouts," Liam said as he stripped down to his boxers. She stared at him. She wanted to poke fun at him. Say that the magazines apparently didn't know what they were talking about. All the polls had concluded that he wore briefs—which was apparently wrong. But she couldn't find the energy to talk. Or maybe she'd forgotten how to form words all together. She wasn't sure.

Her eyes widened as he neared her and started to pull her arms up. She knew he was touching her, but she couldn't feel it. It was the strangest experience. Why couldn't she feel his fingers on her skin?

Once her shirt was off, he leaned her back and unbuttoned her pants. It took some shifting until he'd removed them and laid them in front of the fire.

"Come on," he breathed into her ear as he pulled her to standing.

She knew she should have been able to stand, but every time she tried, her legs collapsed underneath her. Liam steadied his body and swept his arm under her knees, pulling her to his chest.

She rested her body against his as he made his way to the sleeping bag. Her body was no longer numb. It was . . . nothing. It was as if she no longer existed.

"Stay with me," he said as he pulled back the sleeping bag and laid her down.

She was too weak and too numb to feel anything.

"L-L-Liam," she whispered. The warmth of her breath on her

lips shocked her. For a moment, she remembered what it felt like to be warm.

"Don't talk," he said as he climbed in next to her. Reaching over, he zipped the bag closed and pulled her next to him.

He wrapped his arms around her and ducked his head close to her. She could see the rising and falling of his chest. They lay there, not speaking. The only sound that broke up the silence was the crackling of the wood that was only a few feet away from them.

She wanted to talk. She wanted to say something. Thank him for what he'd done. If these were her last moments, she needed him to know that she didn't blame him. That she was the wrong one. She shouldn't have said those things.

"Liam," she whispered again.

"Don't talk," he said. His voice was deep and inches from her ear.

"But, I have—"

"No. This isn't the time. Tell me something else. Tell me a strange fact that I wouldn't know." He tightened his grip on her as he pulled her closer.

Her skin tingled as if it had finally decided to wake up. It was an odd sensation. Like, her body had decided to live and pain was its first reminder.

"But—"

"You can tell me how wrong you were once you're warm. Right now, I just want to hear your voice. Tell me something I don't know." He leaned in, and she could feel his warm breath on her cheek.

She marveled at the feeling of his chest against her arms. She fought the urge to turn her hands outward and feel the warmth of his skin. The warmth of his muscles.

"When someone is lying," she stammered. "Their hands don't move. If they're telling the truth, they move." Her lungs burned as the cool air filled them.

His chest shifted as if he were laughing.

"Really?" he asked.

She nodded.

"What else?"

Why wouldn't he just let her say what she wanted to say? "Liam, I—"

"What else, Ms. Abernathy?"

She closed her eyes and forced another fact to enter her mind. "If you can't sleep, try the 4-7-8 technique. Inhale four seconds. Hold for seven. Exhale for eight."

She felt him take a breath, hold it, and then exhale.

"That works?" he asked.

She nodded into his chest. "It has for me."

He started to pull back, but she wrapped her arm around him, pulling him closer. She wasn't ready to look at him, and she most certainly wasn't ready for him to take away her heat source.

"Sorry. I'll stay put."

She scooted closer—if that were possible. Her skin felt as if it were on fire now. Every part of her was screaming to wake up. She almost missed the feeling of nothingness that freezing brought.

"You okay?" he asked. His voice was husky.

"Yeah. But my skin feels like it's going to crawl off my body."

He wrapped his arm tighter around her. "That's good. It needs to wake up."

"I know," she whispered.

Silence surrounded them once more. The question about his underwear wouldn't leave her alone.

"I have a question."

He kept quiet. "Okay," he finally said.

"I thought you wear briefs."

A rumble rattled around in his chest. "What?"

"Bridget told me you like to wear briefs."

"Oh, she did? Where did she get that idea?"

Madeline spread her fingers out against his chest and marveled at how tan he was against her pale skin. "A magazine."

His muscles tightened against her. She worried, for a moment, that she'd said something wrong.

"We've discussed this. Remember when I said not to trust everything you read in a magazine?"

Madeline tightened as the memory of how Liam felt about reporters rushed through her mind. "Well—"

"Briefs are too tight," he interjected, "against, you know . . ."

She pinched her lips shut as heat raced to her cheeks. Perhaps she should end this conversation before it became too intimate.

"Anything else about me that you think you know?" he asked.

Yes. But she kept her lips pulled taut. At this moment, she didn't want to say anything to upset him. At this moment, she wanted it to be just him and her. Not Madeline and Liam. Not journalist and billionaire. Here, there was no need to think or analyze. Here, they were surviving together. And right now, that was all she needed.

LIAM

An hour had passed, but Liam couldn't calm his mind. Madeline seemed fine. Her eyes were shut, causing her lashes to spread across her cheeks. He shifted and pulled her closer. He wanted to feel her breathing. He couldn't get the image of her limp body from his mind.

His stomach knotted as he loosened his hold on her. Part of him wanted to pull away—to protect himself. The other part never wanted to let go. He wanted to stay here forever wrapped in her arms. He couldn't deny how good her soft skin felt against his. It took all his control not to pull her close and kiss her.

She'd survived. She was okay. His chest swelled as the fear that had rooted itself inside of him released its icy grasp. Even if she had been lying there, spouting ridiculous media reports to him, he wouldn't have it any other way.

She sighed as she shifted. Her eyes fluttered open, and her gaze made its way to him.

"Did I fall asleep?"

He nodded.

"Did you?" she asked.

"I couldn't sleep."

She pulled back a bit and coughed. He furrowed his brow. "You okay?"

"Yeah," she said, covering her mouth.

He nodded as he reached out and brushed a strand of hair from her cheek. "The glacier water is pretty clean, but there could still be a chance of pneumonia. You'll have to tell me if it gets worse, okay?"

Her eyes widened and she nodded. Liam propped himself up on his elbow. Their previous conversation kept playing in his mind. He wondered how many more lies about him she'd bought into. "Are there any more stories about me that I need to set straight?" he asked.

Madeline sighed and shook her head. "No. I've decided to let all of that go. I want to learn about the real Liam. Not the one the media portrays."

His throat caught as he pulled back to look at her. She hesitated but then glanced up to meet his gaze.

"Really?" he asked. He couldn't believe it. Ms. Journalist herself was ready to do some research.

She glared at him. "Don't look so surprised."

He purposely let his jaw hang open. "I'm just . . . shocked."

She smacked his shoulder as she shifted to pull away from him. Not ready to give up his hold her just yet, he reached out and pulled her back. "Where are you going? It's freezing out there. Besides, our clothes aren't dry yet."

She fought it for a moment, before she relaxed. "Fine. I'll stay in here. But you stay on your side, and I'll stay on mine."

"Only you, Ms. Abernathy, could create sides in a sleeping bag." He smiled at her. "As much as I want to honor your decree, it's best for us to stick together. Warmth is a hot commodity in the wilderness." He wiggled closer to her.

She parted her lips but then pinched them together. Her ridged posture relaxed as she nodded. "Fine. But keep your hands to yourself."

"Scout's honor." He smiled as a weight lessened in his chest. He was grateful to see her normal disposition return. That meant she was okay, and that thought made him happier than he'd been in a long time.

They lay there, listening to the wood crackle next to them until Madeline's stomach's growl overpowered the fire. Liam glanced over to her. "Hungry?"

Her cheeks were pink as she nodded. "Yes."

He smiled as he wiggled from the sleeping bag. "I'll brave the cold to get you some food, m'lady," he said, and then paused. "Close your eyes."

Madeline glanced over to him. "Why?"

"I'm only wearing underwear," he whispered, enjoying how her face flushed in response. "And I'm sure if you saw my muscles when you're not fighting for your life, you'd never look at another man again." He lowered his voice as he pulled a serious expression.

Madeline's eyes widened. "You're that confident?"

Liam shifted around and then pulled his arm out from under the sleeping bag. "See these guns? They're just a sample of what's underneath."

Her gaze flickered down to his chest, and for a moment, he could hear his heart pound in his ears. What could she possibly be thinking about for this long? Did he really want to know?

Before they headed into uncharted territory, Liam cleared his throat. "So, for the sake of your sanity, cover your eyes." Or the sake of his stomach, which was now full of butterflies.

She glanced back up at him and then pinched her eyes shut. Liam shifted and scooted and finally emerged from the bag. He curled his body toward itself as he rushed over to his clothes. Thank goodness they were dry.

He shook them out. Once dressed, he stood by the fire with his fingers outstretched. It helped warm his aching body. The sun had disappeared behind the mountain, and the cool temperature was settling in around him. He shivered as he paced up and down the shore. Where had her backpack gone? She'd been the one carrying the food.

"Madeline?" he called out, turning to her lump under the sleeping bag.

She shifted and poked her head out. "What?"

"Where's the backpack?" He stopped and rubbed his face. He couldn't remember seeing her with it when he pulled her from the lake. Duke had finished warming by the fire and joined in his pacing.

Liam glanced down at him. "Where did it go?" he asked.

Duke just cocked his head to the side.

There was a groan from Madeline's direction. "I took it off when I fell into the water. My wallet. My book. My . . ."

Liam glanced over at her. She was studying the lake. Realization dawned on him. The picture of her boyfriend. "Your picture?"

She eyed him. "Yeah," she whispered. "But it's probably for the best."

"What does that mean?"

She squeezed her eyes shut. "Never mind."

Liam didn't want to let it go. But he also didn't want to convince her that he should go into the water to retrieve it. The thought of entering the freezing-cold lake sent shivers down his back. His skin pricked from the memory of the icy water. He couldn't go back into it—no matter what was lost to its depths. "You don't mind if I don't jump in there?"

She shook her head. "No. That would be ridiculous."

He nodded. Well, there was no point in standing out in the elements if there was no food. He whistled for Duke to follow and then headed back to the fire where he stood in front of it with his hands extended.

"I'm sorry for letting the pack go," she whispered.

He turned and shook his head. "Don't worry about. It's better that you live than let that pack drown you."

She stared at the fire. "But if you didn't have me with, you'd have a much better chance at survival."

Liam's stomach tightened. There was truth to her words. Having someone who was inexperienced did hinder things. But he would never admit that he enjoyed her company. That he was starting to wonder if being alone wasn't better.

She scoffed, and he turned to her. What did that mean?

She buried her face under the sleeping bag. "I'm such a joke." Her voice was muffled from the material.

Liam's heart went out to her. Being lost in the wilderness—this was his element. She had to feel so out of control here. He made his way over to where she lay.

"Here I am, writing about everyone else's life when I've barely lived myself." She pulled the cover from her face and jumped when her gaze fell to his. "I mean, I can't even get down a glacier without having it give way underneath me."

Liam squatted down, propping his elbows on top of his knees. "You're not a joke," he said.

She nodded. "Yes, I am. I'm a joke and a sellout. I'm no better than the journalists *The Journal* hired to write 'How to Please Your Man in Ten Moves or Fewer.'" She covered her face with her hands.

Deep down, it felt as if a dagger had been stabbed into his gut. She thought his life story was on the same level of a rubbish article? Writing the story about Davenport Outdoors, although it was to cover up something his father had done, was to save jobs . . . to save him.

He shook his head as he stood. He knew he shouldn't have gotten involved with Madeline. Her pretentious ideas and know-it-all-ness was just going to get him hurt in the end. It was best to stay away from her. Far away.

CHAPTER THIRTEEN

MADELINE

*M*adeline went to bed hungry that night. When she woke up in the morning, her stomach ached. She blinked away the little sleep she'd gotten the night before. The 4-7-8 trick did nothing for her. Not when the sky never truly got dark.

Now she knew why so few people lived here. It was too cold. Too bright. And filled with one particularly hard-to-read billionaire who was curled up next to her.

Even though their conversation had ended abruptly last night, he still insisted they sleep together for warmth. He'd busied himself with building a dome-type shelter while she dressed. Then he told her they should get some sleep. No more in-depth talks. No more shared feelings. It was business as usual.

She sighed as she turned away from Liam. The leaves above her shifted in the breeze. They were a vibrant yellow and contrasted against the blue sky. She stifled a yelp when a wet, cold sensation raced across her cheek. Whipping to the side, she saw Duke's big nose inches from her face.

"Duke!" she hissed, pushing her body farther away from the dog—but not so far that she ran into Liam.

Duke took that as a challenge and scooted closer to her. She pushed away, and panic filled her chest as she scooted right into Liam. He shifted and snuck his arm around her waist. She froze. Crap. What was she supposed to do now?

"Ms. Abernathy," his voice was breathy in her ear.

It sent shivers up her spine. She swallowed. She hated how just two words rendered her speechless. She focused hard and steadied her voice. "What, Mr. Davenport?"

His chest shook from laughter. "If you wanted to snuggle, all you had to do was ask."

Heat raced down her back as she contemplated what was worse. Duke, or lying here, wrapped in Liam's arms. Well, she knew what her heart was saying, but her head won out. She scooted closer to Duke, flinching when his nose brushed her skin again.

"You need to get over that," Liam said. His voice was rough with sleep.

Madeline tried to ignore how close he was to her. "It is a life-long, deep-rooted fear." She flipped to her side so her back was to Duke and there was a good few inches between her body and Liam's.

He'd propped himself up on his elbow and was smiling at her. It must be her desire for food, because her stomach was tied into knots.

"Duke is the nicest dog you'll ever meet. He wouldn't harm a fly." He reached out and ruffled Duke's fur.

Madeline peeked at the animal from over her shoulder. His tongue hung from his mouth as he leaned into Liam's hand. A surge of confidence raced through her as she shifted around and reached out to gingerly placed her hand on Duke's head. The dog whined and nuzzled her.

"See? He likes you," Liam said from behind her. There was laughter in his tone.

Madeline began to stroke the dog's soft fur. Hmm. Perhaps Duke wasn't as bad as she thought. She turned to see Liam staring at her.

His face flushed as he glanced around. "Sleep well?" he asked.

Desperate to get the awkwardness out of the air, Madeline cleared her throat. "No. You snore."

His gaze landed on her. "I do?"

"No one's ever told you?" Liam was a playboy. Certainly, a girl at some point would have told him that he snored.

He pulled at the zipper and flipped the cover open. "I don't have many women sleep in my bed with me," he said as he grabbed his shoes and slipped them on. The fire had burned down to embers.

Madeline pulled the covers tightly around her body, not sure how to interpret what he had just said. Instead of speaking, she watched him stoke the fire. After a few minutes, it roared back to life. She could feel the warmth from the flames on her face.

When she was confident that she wouldn't freeze in the outside world, she got out of the sleeping bag and stood. Her legs were weak, but she forced strength into them. She wasn't going to be one of those desperate women who needed a guy like Liam to survive. She wasn't going to bring him down. There had to be a way for her to be an asset to their journey.

When she took a step toward the fire, her knee buckled, and it felt as if she were falling in slow motion. The ground neared, and there was nothing she could do about it.

Before her body slammed into the ground, she was suddenly weightless. It took a moment for her mind to catch up with what had happened. Liam's arms were wrapped around her once more this morning. He'd pulled her to his chest.

"Whoa," he said, peering down at her.

When she saw the concern in his eyes, she groaned. He tipped his head to the side as he quirked an eyebrow.

"That wasn't the reaction I was expecting from someone who had just been saved from face-planting into the fire," he said.

Too ashamed to look at him, she buried her face into his shoulder. Man, he smelled good. The lake water from the day before had washed away all the expensive cologne from his clothes and exposed something earthy and natural and 100 percent Liam.

Being this close to him sent warning signals to her mind. She wiggled until he set her down. "I'm sorry," she said, trying to hide the frustration from her tone.

"It's okay. It wasn't like you tried to collapse."

She pushed away from him and shook her head. "No. It's me. I'm ridiculous. I promised myself I wasn't going to be a burden, and here I go, falling like some damsel in distress."

He was quiet, so she glanced over to him. Why wasn't he saying anything?

"It's okay not to be amazing at everything. Sometimes it's good to let others help you."

She held up her hand. He needed to stop. "No. I'm not that person. Let's just move forward." She forced a weak smile. Anything to get them talking about something different.

She found a nearby rock and settled down on it. She pulled her clothes closer to her body and glanced around. "So, what's the plan for today?"

"Well, I was thinking we should pack up and get some mileage behind us, but now . . ." He eyed her.

"What?"

He sighed. "Well, I'm thinking we need to get some food first."

Madeline's stomach growled in response, but she shook her head. "No. It's probably better that we get moving. I'm excited to see civilization and flushing toilets."

An expression passed over Liam's face that told Madeline he

doubted they would find those any time soon. But she just waved it away. She wasn't going to think like that right now.

She stood. "All right. Tell me what to do so we can get out of this God-forsaken wilderness."

LIAM

The thicket was dense around them as they stood at the tree line. It had taken over an hour to clear the mountains and arrive at the start of the forest. Thick fog was rolling in around them, but Liam could see down the hill to what looked like a deep gorge. He felt a little hope. That could mean a river was down there.

He stopped and slung his pack off. He straightened, popping his back as he stretched. He'd given the flare gun and bear spray to Madeline. It helped his joints to only have his pack and rifle to carry.

Duke was wandering around, sniffing at things. Madeline glanced over at Liam. Her expression was pained for a moment before she forced a smile.

"Where to?" she asked.

Liam studied her. Why did she have to act so tough all the time? He didn't care that she was out of her element. In fact, he enjoyed taking care of her. He just wished she'd put her pride down long enough to let him in.

"We're going to head down the hill. Hopefully, there's a river down there. Once we make it, we can stop. Then, I'll hunt for some food." He pulled out a water bottle and handed it over to her.

She took it and brought it to her lips. He tried to ignore how tantalizing her neck looked as she tipped her head back. Memories of her body pressed against his entered his mind. He cleared his throat and dropped his gaze. Best to focus on something else.

If she noticed the heat that raced across his skin, she didn't show it. Instead, she handed the water bottle back.

"Okay. Let's do this," she said.

He peeked over to her, wondering how to ask the question that was forming in his mind. Before he chickened out, he decided that being direct was the best policy. "Do you need us to wait a bit longer?"

Her expression hardened as she glanced over to him. "Why would I need to wait longer?"

He sighed, tired of her insistence that being vulnerable was a sign of weakness. "You almost died yesterday." His chest tightened at the thought. "It's okay to need help."

Her gaze softened as she studied him. Then, her shoulders slumped as she glanced around. "I know."

He reached out and brushed his fingers against her shoulder. "I'm sorry you lost all of your belongings."

She glanced over at him as if she'd just remembered that her things were gone. "Oh." She shrugged. "That's okay. It was just underwear and stuff."

He studied her. "Yeah. And the picture of you and your boyfriend." Liam paused. "What's his name?"

She reached out and massaged her calf. "Brett."

"And you've been dating him for three years?"

She was quiet. After a few seconds, she nodded. "Yep."

Liam twisted the cap off the water bottle and took a drink. Why did it bother him so much that this guy would date Madeline for three years? That seemed like forever. Granted, he'd never gotten engaged. Or even gotten close. He usually knew within the first few months if a relationship was going to work out. He would cut the girl loose when that happened.

"What?" Her question broke into his thoughts.

"What's what?"

"You have a weird look on your face." She straightened and glanced around.

"Just seems weird that you've been dating this guy for years and he hasn't pushed the relationships forward."

She coughed. "Like to marriage?"

Liam nodded. "Or is that not part of your life plan?"

Madeline twisted her toe in the gravel at her feet. "No. I want to get married."

For some reason, that statement caused Liam's heart to race, so he turned his attention to the yellow and red leaves that spanned out in front of him. "Alaska is beautiful," he said, hoping to change the subject.

"What about you?"

Crap. She wasn't going to leave it alone. "Me and marriage?"

She wrapped her arms around her chest and nodded. "Yeah. From what I've read, you're quite the player."

Liam laughed. What a joke. That was a magazine's desperate attempt to sell subscriptions.

Madeline's eyes widened. "That's not true?"

He shook his head. "I wish. They make me out to be much more of a player than I actually am." He chuckled as he shoved his hands into his pockets. "They make my life much more interesting than it actually is."

"So, no girls waiting for you on every continent?" Her cheeks flushed, and for a moment that intrigued him.

"No. No girls. I've got no one waiting for me." The words were meant to come out relaxed, but the thought of being alone tugged at his chest, so he dropped his gaze. It was better that he was alone. There was no one to disappoint. He cleared his throat and shifted. He was ready to get moving again.

"You feeling better?" Liam asked.

Madeline studied him. It made him feel exposed. Had he confessed to too much? What was she thinking? He wished he could read her.

"Brett isn't my boyfriend," she said, her voice low.

Liam leaned forward. "What?" Had he heard her right?

"Brett. He's not my boyfriend. In fact, I have no idea where he is. He's my ex-fiancé. He left me a month before the wedding." She glanced down at her hands in her lap.

Liam watched her. Why had she lied to him? Why was she still carrying his picture around with her? And why did he want to punch the guy in the face? "He left you?"

She nodded. "He said he needed to find himself. Bridget said I should move on and hoped that I might be able to do that during this trip. She insisted that I bring the picture to destroy it at some point." She covered her face with her hands. "I'm such a loser."

Liam kicked a stick. "You're not a loser. That guy's a loser. You're better off without him."

She pinched her lips together as she studied him. An uncomfortable look passed over her face. She shook her head and then pushed off the rock. "Let's get going."

Liam paused. He wanted to talk more about this, but Madeline looked as if she wanted to drop the conversation. So he nodded and whistled to Duke who was sitting a few feet away, panting and glancing around. They gathered their items and started into the tree line.

Just as they entered into the forest, a crack rang out in the air. Liam jumped and turned. Madeline had the flare gun raised. Smoke trailed upward as the flare raced into the sky.

"What are you doing?" he gasped. Why on earth would she shoot the flare?

Her hands shook as she pointed upward. He followed her gesture. A tiny speck was making its way across the sky. It was a commercial plane.

"You were signaling that plane?" His mind was trying to catch up with what had happened.

She smiled. "We're saved!"

Liam sputtered. "That's a commercial plane. They fly 30,000 feet up. They're never going to see the flare." He stepped toward her hand reached his hand out. "I can't believe you wasted a flare for that."

Madeline's cheeks heated as she stared at his open hand. "How was I supposed to know?"

Liam wiggled his fingers. "I trusted you," he whispered as she placed the gun into his hand.

"I—" she started.

When he looked up at her, he saw that her jaw had set. Regret filled his chest. He shouldn't have been so hard on her. She really didn't know. "I didn't mean to come down so hard on you. But we only had two flares. And, now, we only have one."

Madeline just nodded as she wrapped her arms around her chest. Liam sighed. It felt as if the connection that they had just had suddenly withered and died. Why did he have to come down so hard on her? Man, he could be a jerk sometimes.

"I'm sorry," he tried again.

She shrugged. "Let's just move on."

He nodded as he shoved the gun into his jacket pocket.

They turned toward the woods and allowed the foliage to swallow them up as they continued on. Soon, he became too preoccupied with navigating the terrain than thinking about their earlier conversation. He tried as hard as he could to guide them around the devil's club, a thorny plant that the natives revered for its medicinal use, but it was everywhere.

Madeline swore under her breath as they entered each patch. Duke had given up and wandered away. Liam thought about calling him back but decided against it. He was a dog. Best to let him do what he wanted.

The farther they got, the more Liam grew uneasy. This was bear country, and most bear attacks came from a startled animal. He glanced back to Madeline who was red-faced and sweaty. She'd pulled her hair up into a bun, but a few curly strands had been set free and surrounded her face. When she glanced up to look at him, his heart raced. Her frustrated gaze caused her green eyes to sparkle. It was an odd sensation.

"So, tell me about your obsession of saying random things,"

Liam said, raising his voice as he turned and pushed through the large leaves that surrounded them. It was best to make as much noise as possible.

"Why are you yelling?"

"To ward off bears. They attack when they're startled."

When Madeline remained quiet, Liam looked back at her. She was glancing around with her eyes wide.

"Don't worry. If we talk loud, we should be fine."

Madeline looked back at him as she bit her lip.

"Come on," he said, waving for her to follow.

He could hear her smacking the foliage behind him.

"So?" he asked.

"So, what?"

"Why do you have this obsessive need to repeat information when you're nervous?" He paused. "Do you have any other strange quirks? Like, do you need to flip the light switch a certain amount of times?"

She scoffed. "No. Nothing like that . . ." Her voice trailed off.

For a moment, Liam worried he'd said something wrong. But then brushed it off. "Madeline? We should talk. You know— bears." He pushed a branch away and held it for her as she walked past.

"I guess I just don't understand why we have to talk about that," she shouted.

Liam stared at her back as he followed behind her. There was something there. Something that she didn't want to talk about. He contemplated asking her more questions. After all, hadn't she pushed him about his father's funeral? Instead, he bit the inside of his cheek and decided to change the subject.

Perhaps, she just needed a bit more time to trust him with personal information. And from the expansiveness of the wilderness that surrounded him, time was all they had.

CHAPTER FOURTEEN

MADELINE

Madeline hated Alaska. She hated plants. She hated the constant drizzle of rain that wasn't going away. And she hated Liam and his pesky questions. Since she'd refused to answer his questions about her parents, he'd decided to focus on her job, her hobbies, and Bridget.

She would have just brushed him off, but facing a ten-foot grizzly bear because she refused to talk didn't seem like a better trade. So, she reluctantly shared almost every aspect of her life with the chatty billionaire behind her.

There was another point for her to add to her article. The Davenports were nosy. While they refused to share personal information about themselves, they loved to find out everything about you. She could work that part into the story. Her lips twitched. It was starting to take a life of its own.

It wasn't until well after noon that they finally broke through the thicket of brush to discover the river that Liam had suspected ran through the gorge. Madeline rejoiced as she knelt by the river and rubbed the cool water all over her face. Her lips tasted salty as she licked them.

When she pushed back onto her knees, she glanced to the side. Liam was unpacking his bag while Duke jumped in and out of the water. Suddenly, the thought of tasting the same water that Duke had just leaped in made her stomach churn.

Blast that dog.

She made her way to a downed tree and sat on its trunk. She attempted to look busy but wasn't sure what she was doing so gave up and pulled her knees to her chest and hugged them.

"What are you doing?" she asked as Liam shoved some bullets into his pants pocket and turned.

"I'm going to go hunting," he said as he slung the rifle onto his shoulder and glanced over at her.

At the mention of food, her stomach growled. "How long are you going to be gone?"

Liam looked up at the sky. The dark clouds had parted giving them reprieve from the rain. The sun shone down on them, lighting up the forest floor.

"Hopefully not long. I really want to keep moving."

Madeline nodded, although her aching feet did not agree. Liam walked over and broke a branch off the log she sat on.

"If it takes too long, we'll have to camp here for the night." He handed her to the dried wood. "Make a fire."

She stared at him. He wanted *her* to make a fire? He had more confidence in her survival skills than she did.

"Okay," she said, hoping her voice came out more confident than she felt.

He stared at her. "Want me to give you some pointers?"

She forced a smile. "I think I've got this," she said as she pulled the branch from him.

He gave her a questioning look and then turned and walked a few feet. "Just don't burn the forest down," he said, looking over his shoulder.

Madeline laughed. "I'll be just fine."

Liam's eyebrows went up, but he didn't say anything further. As he turned to the tree line, panic settled in her gut. She didn't want him to leave. Being around him helped her feel safe. After all, the man did save her life yesterday. Had she even thanked him for that? She couldn't remember.

"Thank you," she said, her voice breathy. It was as if the words didn't want to leave her lips.

Liam glanced back at her. "For what?"

"Saving my life yesterday." As much as she wanted to drop her gaze, she couldn't. His penetrating gaze pulled her in and held her hostage.

He took a step forward, and it seemed as if he wanted to reach out, and Madeline sucked in her breath. Before he made contact, he shook his head and dropped his hand.

"It's my responsibility," he said, his voice gruff. He dipped his head, slipped into the foliage, and disappeared from view.

Duke barked at the spot Liam had disappeared into but didn't follow after him.

Shivers raced down her body. The memory of the Liam's arms wrapped around her in the sleeping bag returned to her mind. She shook her head. Hard. He needed to leave her thoughts and her emotions. Right now.

Duke's barking broke through her thoughts. Of course. Yet again, she was the designated dog sitter. Luckily, her fear of Duke seemed to have subsided. Now he was just a nuisance instead of the source of her terrors.

"Come on, boy," she called to him, desperate for a task to keep her mind off Liam. "Let's make a fire."

After thirty minutes of trying to light the blasted wood she'd collected, frustration boiled over, and she threw the flint into the trees. Why couldn't she figure this out?

Her stomach grumbled louder as she tilted her head back and groaned. She missed civilization where food and matches existed.

Where she didn't need to be around Liam all the time. A place where she could run away when things got too intimate. Back home, she would be able to forget about her feelings.

Duke whined as he sat next to her. She reached out and gingerly placed her hand on his head. Well, at least she had Duke. A sob escaped her lips. Those thoughts did not make her feel better.

After allowing herself a few minutes to feel bad for herself, she sighed and stood. Maybe the wood she'd collected was too wet. After all, everything in Alaska seemed wet. Her feet were perpetually cold. It made sleeping last night terrible. And no matter what she did, she couldn't get the chill out of her bones from the water yesterday.

She grabbed the saw from Liam's backpack and headed into the woods. Duke followed after her. She sighed. He wouldn't follow his master, but instead, he hung out with her.

"Why do you stay around that insufferable man?" she asked as she pushed some branches out of the way. At least she could talk to the dog about her nonexistent feelings. He wouldn't judge her. And he wouldn't ever tell Liam.

Duke panted from behind her.

"He's frustrating and aggravating and . . ." She sighed as Liam's face raced through her mind. It was as if he were haunting her. *And challenging everything I thought I knew about the wealthy.* Her stomach twisted at that thought.

First, she allowed Parker to convince her that going along and writing this article for the Davenports was a good idea. Now, it seemed that she was allowing Liam to cloud her judgment. What was this article going to turn into? Just some puff piece about how great Liam was?

Shaking her head, she sighed. She wasn't going to let him change her. She'd write the correct article about the Davenports no matter how much Liam affected her thoughts.

She turned and made her way back to camp. It was better that she finish the article now, before she allowed herself to fall for the charms of a Davenport. When she got back to Liam's pack, she located her notebook that, thankfully, she'd had him store for her and got started.

The sun dipped behind the trees when she shook her hand out. She'd been writing nonstop, and her fingers were cramping. Man, writing by hand was a lot harder than typing on her computer.

Duke had curled up next to her leg. His chest rose and fell and every so often, a snore escaped his lips. She patted him, thankful for the warmth he gave her.

Replacing the cap on her pen, she shoved it into the binding of her notebook. Then, she ripped the paper out and tucked it into the back of her pants. The article she'd written was concise and accurate. And was probably not something she wanted to show Liam. At least, not until she no longer depended on his know-how to get out of the wilderness.

A weight felt as if it had been lifted from her chest even if a little guilt lingered. Writing the article did help remind her why she had reservations toward Liam from the beginning. Why she needed to keep him at arm's length.

She needed to guard herself. After all, jumping into a relationship feet first is what got her in trouble with Brett. And she'd promised herself when he broke her heart that she would never do that again. Thinking about playboy Liam was not going to help her keep her promise to herself. She needed her mind to keep her heart in check.

The cool air settled around her as she pulled her coat closer to her body. Where was Liam? Why was he taking so long? She glanced upward, wishing she was one of those people who could tell the time by the setting sun. All she saw was pale purples and oranges that streaked the sky. He said he would only be a little while. She swallowed as her heart picked up speed. She needed to calm down. He was fine. She was just being ridiculous.

The leaves rustled above her as the wind danced through

them. She glanced at the sad pile of wood she'd collected with the intention of starting a fire. Right now, a roaring fire sounded amazing. She shivered as she walked over to find the discarded flint. It was a distraction from worrying about Liam. Even if she sucked at making a fire.

Kneeling in front of the wood, she struck the flint. It sparked but did nothing. She shifted the wood and tried again. She'd figure this out. She had to. She couldn't allow her thoughts to return to Liam. Even if her heart pounded so loudly she could hear it in her ears. She needed to keep her mind off him.

LIAM

Liam tried not to give into the frustration that was erupting inside of his stomach. He'd spent all evening tracking what he thought was a herd of deer, only to have the trail go cold. Now, he was miles from camp and it was getting dark.

Not to mention, he had no food.

A rustling in the trees above him caused him to slow and crouch behind a bush. As he peered up, he saw a squirrel jumping through the treetops. Slipping the rifle from his arm, he brought it up to his shoulder. It was food, and he was starving.

He braced himself as he pulled the trigger and the shot rang out. Instantly, the squirrel fell from the tree and landed on the ground in front of him. He grabbed it and tied its leg to the string he'd brought with. One more, and they'd be set for dinner.

Dusk surrounded him as he made his way back to camp. Luckily, he'd left marks on the trees, which lead him back. Without them, there was no way he'd be able to find his way. Everything looked the same.

After he shot another squirrel, he quickened his pace. As he neared the camp, he strained to see through the foliage. There was no glow from a roaring fire. His stomach twisted as fear raced through his mind. Where was Madeline?

When he broke through the tree line, he glanced around. Where was she?

Duke barked and bounded over to him. Liam reached down and tousled the dog's fur. "Where is she?" he asked, trying to keep the concern from his voice.

Duke cocked his head to the side.

"Did she leave you here?" That was his lame attempt at trying to lighten the sinking feeling he had in his stomach. Suddenly, he cursed himself. Why did he leave her alone? She didn't know what she was doing. And she'd almost died yesterday. Liam pushed his hand through his hair as he rested the rifle against a nearby tree and glanced around.

"Madeline?"

Nothing.

His heart pounded so hard it felt as if it was going to jump from his chest and take off. She had to be okay. She just had to.

"Where is she, boy?" he asked Duke who was following behind him as he paced around the camp.

Duke didn't respond.

"Madeline?"

A rustling sounded to his left. He whipped around, now regretting not having a gun with him. But, perhaps, that was best. Right now, he was so jumpy he might accidentally shoot when it's not be necessary.

The noise grew louder. Liam readied his stance for whatever creature was about to burst through the foliage. He kept silent as he waited. Hoping to get the jump on the animal.

As the creature emerged, Liam raced toward it. It turned and its gaze met his. It was Madeline. Her eyes widened. She screamed and dropped the pile of wood that she was cradling in her arms.

"What are you doing?" she asked as she raised her hands.

Relief flooded Liam's chest. She was safe. Granted, a little terrified, but she was okay. He reached out and grabbed her arms and pulled her to his chest.

"I thought an animal got to you," he said as he allowed the feeling of her body next to his rush over him.

"Liam," she whispered as she pressed her hands against his chest and pulled back. "You're crushing me."

"Oh, sorry," he said as he glanced down at her. Big mistake. She too close. He could just reach down and brush his lips against hers. And he wanted to. Man, did he want to.

CHAPTER FIFTEEN

MADELINE

*L*iam was close. Too close. Part of her wanted to stay wrapped up in his arms, but the other part of her wanted to run. She was getting too attached. She should know better.

But she had become so worried that something might have happened to him that being in his presence soothed the ache in her soul. He peered down at her with such a serious expression that she almost leaned in. Almost.

Thankfully, her head was louder than her heart. Taking the moment of strength that she had, she pulled back far enough to break his hold on her. The cool evening air whipped around her, reminding her just how chilly it was to be alone in the Alaskan wilderness.

"Are you okay?" Liam asked. His voice deeper than normal. It sent shivers down her spine.

She nodded and bit her lip. They needed to put distance between them. Now. "What took you so long?" she asked, hoping the coolness in her voice helped to calm her pounding heart.

He quirked an eyebrow. "What do you mean?"

"You were gone all evening. I thought you wanted to keep moving. Now it looks like we're going to have to set up camp."

He took a step back. "Well, I was out trying to kill dinner. What about you? Looks like you got . . ."—his gaze swept over the campsite—"nothing done."

"Well, I . . ." Heat pricked Madeline's neck. Good. Frustration helped to push out the ridiculous feelings of infatuation she was feeling. Because she couldn't get deep feelings for Liam Davenport. That was ridiculous. "I tried to start a fire, but the stupid thing you gave me to use didn't work." She dug into her pocket for the flint and handed it over.

Liam stared at it and then his gaze raced up her arm to her face. "You spent this entire time I was gone trying to light the fire? Where's the wood?" He took a few steps over to her meager pile and picked it up. "Of course it's not going to light. This is damp."

"The whole forest is damp!" she said, waving her arms around. The drizzle had started again. The droplets landed on her head and raced down her back.

"If we're going to survive, you are going to have to pull your weight."

Oh. No. That was the wrong thing for him to say. "I pull my weight."

Liam tilted his head. "Uh huh," he said as he began walking around, taking stock of the tree branches around them.

There was no way Liam was going to build a fire before her. She had to prove herself. She wasn't weak. And there was no way she was going to let him think that.

Finally, they both came back to the center of the clearing with piles of wood in their arms. Liam dumped his down and began leaning them together in a teepee fashion. Madeline harrumphed as she started to build a log cabin.

In a matter of moments, Liam's fire was raging while all Madeline could get was a tiny spark that dwindled down to nothing.

She tried to swallow her pride, but she couldn't help it—she was disappointed.

She crouched down in front of her pile and kept rubbing the flint stick over and over again, just to watch the spark die within seconds. Tears brimmed her eyelids as she refused to look up. There was no way she wanted to see the triumphant look on Liam's face.

"Do you want some help?" his deep voice asked from behind her, causing her to jump.

She kept her head down as she shook it. "No."

Seconds ticked by, but they felt like hours. Finally, two arms appeared on both sides of her as Liam wrapped his hands around hers.

"You need to get closer to the tampon," he said, his breath tickling her ear.

His nearness paralyzed her limbs. All she could do was nod. He brought the flint stick up and scraped it against the other. The spark shot from it and landed on the cotton.

It ignited it for a moment before a raindrop put it out.

"Try again," he said, never taking his hands away.

Madeline crouched closer to the wood and repeated the steps. All the while, Liam's body remained pressed against hers. After a few more strikes, the cotton ignited and so did the rest of the kindling she'd gathered. As the flames licked the wood, Liam released her and sat back.

She glanced over to him. He was studying her in a way that told her she really didn't want to know what he was thinking. She doubted she could digest his thoughts right now.

"Why do you do that?" he asked as he leaned on one elbow and stretched out his legs.

"Do what?" She threw some more wood onto the flames, which ate them up gleefully. There was something soothing about a fire. It helped warm her body in the absence of Liam. She shook her head. The thought of him pressed against her needed to leave. Now.

"Act so strong all the time? Never let anyone help you?"

"I let people help me."

When he didn't respond, she snuck another look. He had his eyebrows raised.

"You don't believe me?"

Liam smiled. That blasted half-smile. "No. I don't believe you."

Madeline picked some bark off a branch and threw it into the fire. "I don't know."

From the corner of her eyes, she saw Liam straighten. "See, now, I think you do. Back at the plane, you reamed me out about not wanting to attend my father's funeral, but here you sit, as distant to the people around you as I am." He wrapped his arm around his knee and stared over at her.

"I'm not distant."

Liam scoffed. "Sure."

"I'm not. Ask me any question, and I'll answer it." As soon as she spoke the words, she regretted them. Did she really want to bare her soul to him? What would he do with that information?

"Okay. Tell me about your parents."

Her stomach felt like lead in her body. Why did she have to make that promise? Bridget didn't even know everything about her. "I don't want to talk about that," she said as she stood and made her way over to tree line.

There was a rustling sound followed by footsteps. She could feel Liam as he came up from behind her. Her body longed for his arms to wrap around her again. Stupid body.

"Just as I thought. You're so guarded. And, yet you had the gall to chasten me."

Anger exploded from her spine as she whipped around. "Don't talk to me like you know me." She desperately fought the tears that threatened to spill. She couldn't appear weak in front of him. She needed to be strong. She always needed to be strong.

He leaned back a bit, as if he hadn't meant to make her so angry. "Why won't you let me know you?"

She clenched her jaw as she turned back to stare at the tree trunks in front of her. "Because, you'll leave," she whispered. Finally, the truth. It was like a weight was lifted from her chest, and she could breathe. And yet, it terrified her.

A warm hand engulfed her elbow. She shivered as he pulled her around. She was inches from him. There was something so familiar about being this close to him. And she longed for that familiarity.

"Why would you think I would leave you?" His voice was husky as he stepped closer to her.

"Because everyone leaves me. I'm alone. Now and always." She couldn't meet his gaze. Here, staring at the ground, she was safe.

His finger pressed under her chin as he pushed it upward, forcing her to look into his eyes. "Madeline." He whispered.

She kept her gaze down for as long as she could. When she looked up, she cursed herself for doing it. His gaze was full of pain as well. Like he knew exactly what she was going through. A tear slipped down her cheek. He reached up and brushed it with his fingertips.

"Why are you crying?" he whispered.

She closed her eyes, allowing another tear to escape. "I don't want to get hurt." When she opened her eyes back up, Liam was inches from her lips. Her body tingled as he drew closer.

"I won't hurt you, if you don't hurt me," he said, his lips hovering over hers.

"Promise?" If she moved just a tiny bit, her lips would touch his. And she wanted it. Goodness, she wanted it.

"I promise," he said and closed the gap.

Heat rushed to Madeline's stomach as his lips met hers. They were warm against the cool Alaskan air. She pressed her body close to his as she ran her hands up his chest and reveled in the feeling of his taut muscles against her palms. Her hands found their way past his shoulders to the nape of his neck where she tangled her fingers in his hair.

A moan rumbled deep in his throat as he pulled her up. She wrapped her legs around his waist. He moved a foot toward the forest and pressed her back against the nearest tree as if he needed the added strength. Liam remained close, pressing a hand on the trunk behind her. He deepened the kiss, and the feeling of his body against hers took her breath away.

Everything that she thought she knew about Liam flew from her mind. All that remained was the joy that came from kissing him. From being so close to him that she wasn't sure where she ended and he started. As much as it scared her to admit, it felt right. Completely right.

He lowered her legs to the ground as he pulled back and glanced down at her. Her heart ached for him to return. She tried not to groan in protest. When his gaze met hers, she held it, letting him see her. At this moment, she wasn't going to hold anything back.

He leaned forward and kissed her nose, both cheeks, and then softly brushed his lips against hers again.

"I should make you angry more often," he said, his lips centimeters from hers.

"Yeah?"

"You're adorable when you're angry. I can't help myself." He teased her with his lips. He leaned in to kiss her and then pulled away to smile down at her.

Finally, she stood on her tippy toes, wrapping her hands around the back of his neck and pressing her lips against his. She never wanted this moment to end. He reached down and swept his arm under her knees. He pulled her close to his chest as he smiled down at her.

"Where are you taking me?" she asked through her giggles.

He gave her a sly look and leaned in to kiss her. "It's cold," he said as he set her down in front of the fire.

She feigned a hurt look. "My kisses aren't warm enough for you?"

His expression grew serious. "Well, I didn't want to say it . . ."

"Hey!" She smacked his shoulder.

He leaned forward and kissed her again. "Actually, m'lady, I'm going to get started cooking dinner." He nodded toward the squirrels that were in a pile a few feet away.

"That's dinner?" She scrunched her nose up at the sight of them. "Seriously?"

"They don't have McDonald's this far out," he said as he made his way over to them.

Madeline sat back as she watched him prep the animals. She tried not to think too hard about what he was doing. Instead, her thoughts turned to their previous conversation. Suddenly, she wanted him to know the truth.

"My dad used to drink," she said, her voice softer than she intended.

Liam looked up from the squirrel. He studied her but didn't say anything, so she continued.

"He'd come home from the bar totally wasted." She brought up her nail to chew on it. "He wasn't a nice drunk. He was . . . abusive."

An angry expression flashed across Liam's face. "To you?"

Madeline shrugged. "Rarely. Mostly, my mom took the brunt of it. I would hide in my room and listen to him beat her . . ." The thoughts felt as raw as the times it happened. As if speaking the words breathed life into the memory.

"You don't have to continue if you don't want to." Liam had stopped skinning the animal and leaned toward her.

Madeline shook her head. "I want to." She took in a deep breath. "I would hide under my bed and plug my ears to drown out their fights." She closed her eyes. She could still feel the coolness of the hardwood floor beneath her.

"That's why you say random things when you're nervous."

Madeline nodded. "They died when I was sixteen. Car accident."

Liam's expression softened. "Both?"

"Yes. I lived with my aunt until I was eighteen and have been on my own since."

Liam dropped his knife and made his way over to her. He kept his hands up but leaned in and kissed her gently on the lips. When he pulled away, he met her gaze. "I'm so sorry."

She shrugged. "It's okay. It's in the past."

"I will never hurt you," he said, leaning in to kiss her.

As much as she wanted to believe him, doubt lingered in the back of her mind. Men always disappointed her. What made this billionaire any different?

LIAM

Once the squirrels were cooked and eaten, Liam gathered up their items. "We should get going," he said.

She stared at him as if he were joking. "What?"

Liam tied up the pack and whistled to Duke. "We can't stay where we cooked our food. Bears." He nodded into the woods.

Her eyes widened. "You think it's best?"

"Unless you want to share your space with a giant hungry grizzly, we can't stay here," Liam said. "We'll set up camp farther down."

She groaned. He took this time to wrap his arm around her waist and draw her closer. His heart quickened at the closeness of her body. He still couldn't get over how kissing her completed him. For the first time in a long time, he felt happy. Plus, she'd decided to confide in him. That thought made his heart swell. She'd decided to trust him. He couldn't ask for anything more. Well, maybe a shower and his bed.

"It's okay. I promised I'd keep you safe, and this is how." He glanced down at her and smiled.

Madeline's shoulders loosened as she looked up at him. "Okay."

It took about a half an hour to move and get everything unpacked at the new campsite. He was grateful for the distraction that building a dome structure for them to sleep under brought. The memory of their kiss still lingered in his mind and on his lips. His body ached to bring her near again.

But could he do that? Just walk up and kiss her? She didn't seem to protest the previous kiss, but did that mean she would be okay with future ones?

He stifled a groan as he gathered some spruce branches to make a roof. This was not what he wanted. It felt so grade school. Passing notes to each other to see if the other person liked you.

As he finished stacking the branches on the roof, he sighed. It would be best to just come right out and ask her. He allowed his gaze to find its way over to where she sat. She had her knees pulled up, and she was staring into the fire in front of her. The glow danced across her skin.

His chest tightened as he dropped his gaze. He wanted to know what that kiss meant. If she felt the way he did. He wanted to open his heart up to her, and for her to do the same. But if she rejected him, he wasn't sure he could handle the heartbreak.

He sighed as he took a drink of water. He surveyed his work. Exhaustion flooded his body. He needed to stop thinking and get some rest. Tomorrow he'd dissect her intentions. But for now, they'd sleep.

CHAPTER SIXTEEN

MADELINE

*L*iam didn't talk about the kiss the rest of the night. In fact, he didn't move to kiss her again. It was if their previous campsite held all the magic, and at the new place, it was business as usual.

His soft breathing could be heard millimeters from where she lay. Even though they hadn't kissed again, he'd thought it would be a good idea if they slept in the same sleeping bag. That way, they could share body warmth and be close to one another in case something decided to burst from the woods and attack them.

What he didn't mention was being this close to him without knowing what they were was pure torture for Madeline. But she felt stupid for asking. Who does that nowadays? Having a discussion to determine the relationship? Man, she'd sound like a loser.

Flipping to her side, she wrapped her arms around her chest. She started taking in deep breaths, holding them, and then releasing them out. She willed her body to relax and, soon, it did what it was told.

The sun peeked into the small hut-like structure Liam had

built. Madeline squeezed her eyes shut. She wasn't quite ready to wake up yet. It felt as if she'd just fallen asleep. Groaning, she flipped to her stomach and buried her face in the sleeping bag.

Reaching out, she felt around for Liam. Of course he was gone. Why would he hang out in a sleeping bag with the woman he'd just shared a mind-blowing kiss with? She tapped her head with her fingers, hoping it would remove the memory of his lips pressed to hers. She desperately wanted their relationship to go back to normal. Right?

No longer able to sleep, Madeline flung the covers from her body and sat up. The fire had died down to a steady burn. Duke lay next to it, his head in his paws. She didn't see Liam. Where was he?

Rustling in the leaves next to her caused her heart to pick up speed. She breathed out as she steadied her nerves. It was just Liam. That was all.

Duke scrambled to his feet. His bark rang out against the morning air. Heat pricked Madeline's spine as she stared at the dog. Did he know something she didn't?

"Duke, hush!" she said. If it was an animal, she didn't want the stupid dog to draw it closer.

Duke didn't relent. His barks grew deeper as his upper lip curled back. Madeline's heart pounded. It wasn't Liam. It was something else. Tucking her legs against her body, she hid inside the structure.

The rustling grew louder, followed by a deep growl. Her heart stopped as a giant brown bear emerged from behind the leaves. Duke continued to bark as he backed up.

The bear looked around as it crept out of the tree line and into their camp. She stifled a whimper as it lifted its nose into the air. She could see its nostrils flare as it moved its head from side to side.

Pressing her mouth into her knees, she swallowed hard against the fear that exploded in her chest. Duke seemed to have found his strength and approached the bear. His lips were raised, exposing his teeth.

Madeline chanted in her mind for Duke to back off. She didn't love the dog, but she didn't want to see him get hurt. But telepathy must not work on animals. Duke remained vigilant, every so often, gathering enough courage to lunge at the bear.

She watched with wide eyes as the bear strolled through camp as if it owned the place. It paid no mind to Duke. It was as if Duke, who had terrified her when she first met him, was merely a pesky flea that the bear didn't even care enough to scratch at.

Perhaps, if she remained silent, the bear would grow bored and leave. Just when she allowed herself to hope, Duke lunged forward and snapped at the bear's front paw, and the bear let out a deep bark-like growl

Somewhere deep inside, a crazy person exploded out of Madeline. Duke was in trouble. She whipped the blankets off her lap and leaped from the dome. Her hands were outstretched. Why were her hands outstretched? What was she going to do against a grizzly?

The bear whipped his head in her direction, and her heart sank. His growl turned deeper as he rose up on his hind legs.

"Duke. Run!" she screamed. She did the only thing she could think of: she dropped to the ground. Her body shook as she covered her head with her hands and waited for the strike.

But it didn't come.

Instead, Duke's growl sounded first, followed by a whimper. She could hear a tussle above her, but she was too scared to look up. From the sounds above her, she knew they were fighting, and she feared the outcome.

The same heart-pounding, gut-wrenching emotions raced through her. This was all too familiar. Once again, she was a little kid, hiding under her bed, listening to her father attack her mother. And there was nothing she could do about it.

Her hearing dulled as she squeezed her eyes tighter. She willed her body to stop shaking. She willed her heart to calm. She was no use to anyone. Not even Duke.

A gunshot cut through the air. She lifted her head to see Liam rush from the woods. He was shouting something at her, but she couldn't make out the words. Her ears rang, muting any sound.

He motioned toward the retreating bear and then waved at her to get up. The signals made sense, but her body wasn't processing them. She watched as he knelt down next to Duke's crumpled body.

The look of devastation told her everything she needed to know and everything she feared. He was dead. Gone. Killed trying to protect her.

Her chest heaved as sobs escaped her lips. Duke was dead. Yet another in her life who died because she was weak. She buried her face in her hands. Why did she leave the shelter? The bear seemed less threatened by Duke than her. It was her fault he was dead.

Her body felt heavy as she lay on the grass. What was Liam going to say to her? She killed his dog. His best friend. She wouldn't be surprised if he left her to fend for herself in the wilderness. After all, it seemed the only thing she was good for was slowing him down.

"Are you hurt?" Liam's frantic voice ripped through her thoughts as he shook her shoulder.

Turning her head to the side, she glanced over at him. "What?" she asked. Her eyes were puffy and could barely make out his features.

"I said, are you hurt?"

Madeline turned her face back to the ground. "No," she whispered. But she should be.

LIAM

There were too many emotions racing through Liam's body to comprehend any of them. There had been a bear. Duke was severely injured. And Madeline was crumbled on the ground, and her whole body was shaking.

Overwhelmed with what to do first, Liam let his natural instinct kick in. He laid his gun against a tree and made his way over to Madeline. He needed her to gather her wits and help him. Most of the lacerations Duke endured weren't that deep. But there was one that was oozing blood. He reached out and shook her shoulder. She turned to look at him. Her eyes were red and dirt streaked across her cheek.

His pulse quickened. Did the bear get to her as well?

Her face disappeared as she turned her head back to the ground. "Leave me alone," she whispered.

Liam had seen this before. She was in shock. He needed to visually make sure she was safe. He pushed her over. Her fiery gaze met his as he stretched her legs out. There was not time to waste. If she was injured, he needed to know now.

"What are you doing?" she asked, trying to get up.

"I need to see that you are okay."

She pulled her jacket closer to her body as she inched away from him. "I said I was fine."

Liam was tired of her stubbornness. "No. What you said was that you weren't hurt. I need to make sure that's true." His gaze swept over her. Relief filled his chest when he didn't see any blood. She seemed to have control over her limbs. She was using her arms and legs to scramble to her feet.

"I said I was fine." She wrapped her arms around her chest as her face crinkled. He could tell she was fighting not to look in Duke's direction.

She turned and stumbled over to a log that Liam had dragged to the fire the night before. She collapsed on it and tilted her head up to the sky.

"Good. Duke needs your help," Liam said.

Her expression soured as she glanced over to him. "That's not funny."

Not wanting to waste any more time trying to figure out what she was talking about, Liam made his way over to his pack and pulled it open. He fished around until he found the sewing kit he'd grabbed from the plane.

"I'm not sure what you're talking about, but Duke needs our help." He waved at her to follow as he walked past her and over to Duke.

He knelt down in front of his dog, who moved his head slightly toward him. "It's okay, boy. I'm here." He stifled the tears that brimmed his eyelids. He shook his head hard. This wasn't the time to let his emotions spill over. Duke needed him.

Madeline's shadow cast over them as she stood next to him. "Duke's not dead?" she asked in hushed tones.

"He will be if I don't close up this wound." He waved to the blood that had matted down the fur.

Madeline dropped to the ground and reached out to pet Duke's head. "He saved me," she whispered.

Liam glanced over to her. "Then get it together and save him."

Her eyes widened as she glanced up at him. A stony expression hardened her gaze. "Okay," she said. "Tell me what to do."

Liam had Madeline hold Duke still as he worked on cleaning up the cut. Duke fought it at first but soon grew limp. He must have passed out from the pain. For a moment, Liam worried Duke was gone, but relief flooded his body when he saw the dogs labored but distinct breaths.

Once he was finished, he rocked back onto his heels. He'd done all he could. It was up to Duke now. He held his hands up. Duke's blood was all over his skin. Every time he looked at it, he wanted to hurl. He needed to wash it off. Now.

"I'm going to go wash my hands," he murmured as he stumbled away from Madeline. She was crouched next to Duke, rubbing his head over and over again.

It felt like an eternity until he found the river and dropped to his knees in front of it. He dipped his hands into the frigid water.

It rushed over his skin, taking the blood with it. He stared at it, and then his stomach heaved.

Once his body had expelled the last of his stomachs contents, he sat back, not caring if the water soaked his clothes. Duke was injured. Badly. What if he didn't pull through? What if he was gone? Liam would do anything to reverse time and stay instead of hunting this morning. Perhaps, if he hadn't left, Duke wouldn't be hanging on to life by a small thread.

His shoulders shook as he covered his face with his hands. Yet again, he'd made the wrong choice and people got hurt. He couldn't save anyone. He was a fool to think it was wise to get close to anyone. Why he thought things had changed boggled his mind.

He stared out to the river, the sound of its movement filling his ears. He should be alone. No one got hurt when he was alone.

After he composed himself, he stood and made his way back to the campsite. Madeline had moved about a foot from Duke, and she was hunched over, staring at a piece of paper. He paused. What was that?

Shaking his head, he pushed through the trees. It was probably nothing. As he studied her, his heart went out to her. She seemed so small. So frail. And he thought it would be okay for him to get involved with her.

The promise he made to her yesterday raced through his mind. He promised to protect her and look—he'd not only crashed a plane with her in it, but now, she'd almost died from a bear attack.

All of this was his fault. It would be better to pull away. Keep her at a distance. It would hurt, but it would be the best thing. For the both of them. He straightened his shoulders and broke through the brush. Madeline jumped as she whipped around to meet his gaze. She dropped the piece of paper behind her. Curiosity got the better of him when he saw her cover it with some fallen leaves.

What was she looking at? She seemed so embarrassed by it.

Brett's picture had been in her pack and that was at the bottom of the glacier lake. So, what was this? He eyed her for a moment and then shook off the feeling of confusion. It was most likely nothing.

"He okay?" he asked as he made his way to Duke.

"I'm not sure," she said. Her voice was weak.

Liam nodded. "You should go get washed off. We need to get moving. I'm not sure if the bear is planning on coming back or not. It's best if we move on."

"Move Duke?" Her eyebrows rose.

"It's not ideal, but we can't stay here. If there's a chance we might reach anyone in the forest, we need to get moving. Now."

"But—"

"Now, Madeline. You've already done enough." The words tasted bitter on his tongue, but this wasn't the time for him to stop and explain everything so she could felt better about it. Besides, they needed to detach themselves from each other.

When he braved a look in her direction, a feeling of satisfaction settled in his stomach. Her lips were pinched together, and her pale skin had been replaced by bright red cheeks. He'd upset her. Good. They just needed to survive until they were found, and then he could disappear and never return.

She stood and folded her arms. "Fine." She huffed as she pushed through the trees and disappeared. When the sound of her footsteps faded, Liam eyed where she'd been sitting before. He reached down and patted Duke's head. He was still alive, thank goodness. Liam felt so weak. There was nothing he could do to pull his dog through. It was up to the will of Duke now.

Desperate for a distraction, Liam made his way over to the small mound of leaves Madeline had placed over the paper and stared down at it. Should he pick it up? It seemed Madeline didn't want him to know it was there.

He turned but paused. Underneath a particularly vibrant red leaf, he saw the letters, *Li*. He peered down at it to get a better look. Was that his name? He glanced around before he nudged the leave with his shoe.

Liam

She wrote something about him. Well, now he had to look. He reached down and picked up the paper, the leaves falling to the ground at his feet. Heat raced from his spine as he read the article that she had scrawled across it.

When he was finished, he clenched his jaw. So this was what Madeline Abernathy really thought of him.

CHAPTER SEVENTEEN

MADELINE

*L*iam was silent when she returned to the campsite. She was shaky, jumping at every sound, but did feel better after having washed her face seven times in the icy water. It took all her courage to go out into the woods by herself, but facing the bear didn't seem as bad as facing the disappointment that was written all over Liam's face.

His words had cut deeper than any words her father ever yelled at her mother, or herself. She'd let him down, and Liam knew it. She steadied her breath as she walked up to him.

"What can I do to help?" she asked.

Liam glanced over to her. His jaw was set, and his gaze lethal. "Grab the sleeping bag." He nodded toward the dome he'd made.

She bit her lip to keep from saying anything and walked past him. Reaching out, she grabbed the bag and began to roll it.

Liam busied himself behind her. She could hear his footsteps as he walked back and forth, laying things out on the tarp. She wanted to say something. Explain what had happened. But the words wouldn't form on her lips.

Instead, she just kept rolling and unrolling the sleeping bag. No matter how hard she tried to keep it tight, the roll seemed to veer off to the side or slip from her fingers. She sighed and glanced up to the sky. She needed to get home and away from Liam. She'd had just about enough heartbreak for one night.

A roaring sound filled the air. Madeline dropped her gaze to look at Liam. Did he hear it too? Or was it just her desperate need for a plane to appear that caused her mind to conjured one up for her?

The joy that flooded Liam's face told her this wasn't her imagination. There was a plane above them. She tilted her face back up and saw the pontoons that hung underneath the plane. It was small, which meant it wasn't that high up.

"Flare!" Liam yelled. He dropped the cooking utensils he had stacked in his arms and scrambled for his jacket.

Madeline lunged for it as well, grabbing onto one of the sleeves to pull it toward her, but Liam had already stepped on it. He fumbled with the pockets and then lifted his arm in triumph. The orange flare gun was clutched in his hand. He raised it to the sky, and she covered her ears. He pulled the trigger back and she winced, waiting for the sound that normally came when something was shot.

But the sound never came. She peered over to Liam who was staring into the sky before he then lowered the gun. He turned his hand to look at it and then smacked it a few times. Cocking the hammer back, he raised it to the sky again and pulled the trigger.

Nothing.

"What's wrong?" Madeline asked as she watched the plane fly from view. They still had a few moments left. It had worked once before. Why wasn't Liam trying to get the gun to work again?

Liam kept his hand in the air as he pulled the hammer back and pulled the trigger. He did it five more times. With each dead click, his face reddened. Finally, he cursed and threw the gun into the woods.

Madeline stared at it. The plane was gone. Again. And they were left in the wilderness. Again.

"Why did you stop?" she asked as she scrambled to her feet and over to the woods where she searched for the gun.

"It's dead," Liam grumbled as he scrubbed his face with his hands.

"But . . ." Madeline stared at the gun and then back to Liam. It was the only thing that could get them rescued. "It can't be dead. It worked once before."

Liam glanced down at her, and his eyes narrowed. "It's dead. D-E-A-D. Dead." He kicked a rock and sent it flying into the trees. He moved back to gather up what he'd dropped.

"Why would you have a flare gun that doesn't work?" she asked, tossing it to the side.

Liam whipped around. "Oh, so now the malfunction of the flare is somehow my fault? I wasn't the one who shot the gun at the commercial plane in the first place." In two steps, he was next to her. She could see his ragged breathing as he stared her down.

She winced. That was true. She had made mistakes, just like him. It was time she started owning up to them, instead of brushing them off. "You're right. I'm sorry. I shouldn't have shot the flare at the commercial plane. I shouldn't have yelled at you just now. And I should have protected Duke." There. She'd said the truth. She opened herself up and forced herself to be vulnerable. Why was her heart pounding so hard?

Liam stared at her. She could feel the confusion in his gaze. He paused before his expression hardened. What did that mean? He pinched his lips together and turned.

"Ms. Abernathy, I think it's best if we don't speak to one another for a while. Let's get packed up and head out of here. Good news, with a plane that low, there's bound to be hunters around. Maybe even a shelter. We should get moving before it gets too dark." He paused and glanced over at her.

Her stomach twisted. She'd been truthful to him and this was all he had to say? Should there have been something more? As she held his gaze, she saw something there. Something he wasn't saying. For a moment, she wanted to know what that was. But then he turned, and she was snapped back to reality. Liam wasn't going to soften or be truthful.

"Fine," she said. Turning on her heel, she headed back over to the sleeping bag and began to roll it.

She could hear Liam's frustrated grunts from behind her. She did feel a bit bad for how she treated him. He really didn't have any idea that the flare wouldn't work. It wasn't as if he was out to sabotage their rescue.

A heavy sigh sounded behind her. She turned and squinted as she looked up at Liam. The sun shone behind him. She lifted up her hand to shield her eyes.

"I just need to take a minute for myself. I'll be back in a few," Liam said.

From the look on his face and the tone in his voice, she decided not to push it. Perhaps, it would be better if they spent more time away from each other.

"Okay," she said.

Liam nodded and then pushed into the woods and disappeared.

Madeline turned her attention back to the sleeping bag and focused all of her energy on getting it put away and secured. Once it was ready, she grabbed it and walked over to the other supplies and rested it next to the tarp.

As she moved to leave, something caught her eye. Turning, she leaned down and her heart stopped. A piece of paper stuck out from underneath some folded clothes. She grabbed the corner and pulled.

It was her article. Crap.

Liam had seen it. He read the words she'd written about him. The awful, terrible things she had said.

She crumpled up the piece of paper and threw it into the

woods. Was that why he'd been so cool to her when she'd returned? It was because he had read her thoughts? That she felt that a Davenport was nothing more than a spoiled citizen who felt as if they were above common decency? That they respected nothing and no one whom they felt was beneath them?

Her stomach twisted as she thought about the other horrible things she had written about him. That she had written about his father. She chewed her lip as she glanced around. True, at the time she had written the words, she was angry with him. She was just getting out her feelings. She hadn't meant the words. But, now, having spent time with Liam and getting to know him, things have changed. Those words no longer felt true.

Desperate for a distraction, Madeline headed over to Duke to see how he was doing. She knelt down beside him and rested her hand on his head. She glanced to his chest and saw it rise and fall. It soothed her to watch. He was still alive. She leaned closer to his ear.

"I'm sorry," she whispered. "I'm sorry I ever judged you before I knew the kind of dog you were. I promise if you make it out of here alive, I will treat you better."

She glanced down at him and, for a moment, let the flicker of hope burn in her heart that her words just might be the key to wake him up. But his eyes remained closed and his breathing labored.

Feeling stupid, she reached down and patted Duke's head. "I'm not sure why I thought that would work." She glanced over to where Liam had disappeared. Perhaps saying she was sorry to Duke made her feel a tiny bit better about what she'd said about Liam.

She sighed as she sat back and crossed her legs in front of her. It was a ridiculous thought. Liam had to be hurt by what she said about him. And rightfully so. She stood and peered past the brush that Liam had disappeared through. Should she follow after him? Tell her she no longer felt that way?

She gnawed on her nail as she paced back and forth. How did she feel about him? If she told him she'd written the wrong thing, he was bound to ask her what the right thing was. Her heart picked up speed as she thought about it. When realization settled around her, her shoulders slumped.

She knew what the right thing was. She had fallen for Liam Davenport. Hard. He challenged her. Made her so mad that sometimes her blood boiled. But in the quiet moments, when her past came back to haunt her or she felt alone and vulnerable, he was there to be a strength. And she needed that strength.

She needed his friendship. If she walked out of this forest without telling him, she'd never forgive herself. Shaking her arms out, she drew in a deep breath. She'd find Liam and tell him. As she let her breath slip through her lips, her stomach twisted. She needed to do it now, before she lost her nerve.

LIAM

The sun burst through the leaves above Liam. Every time the wind blew, it caused the shadows to shift below him. The steady sound of the rushing river filled the air. He had propped himself up against a nearby rock. His arms were folded as he stared out into the expansive woods in front of him.

Madeline's words kept repeating in his mind. Some were sections of her so-called article that reamed out his family and rich people in general. Some were the words she'd spoken to him. And how she'd spoken to him.

He sighed and rubbed his shoulder. There was a knot that had formed there from sleeping on the ground next to her. He rubbed his arm as he thought about the feeling of having her so close to him. Sharing warmth with her.

And the kiss they'd shared last night. The closeness he'd allowed himself to feel. He reached down and grabbed a flat rock.

He angled his body toward the river and chucked it into the water. It plopped and then disappeared.

He was such a fool. He should have never let himself care for Madeline. She was nothing more than a reporter. There was no way he was ever going to change her mind. And he was an idiot to think he could.

He pushed off the rock and stood. Then he swung his arms across his chest, hoping that physical exertion would help calm his pounding heart. It was conflicting with the thoughts that were racing around in his mind.

He jumped a few times. Then growled. Good. This was helping him return to Earth and out of the clouds where he often went when he was around Madeline. There was something about her that drew him in. And he hated how helpless he felt around her. Especially when he'd just read her true feelings about him. Those were something he could never change.

Once he felt that he had his emotions under control, he threw one last rock into the water and then headed back to camp. He walked through the trees, smacking the leaves as he went. Hopefully, that plane they'd seen earlier meant there were hunters around, and perhaps a lodge. He allowed the idea that they just might get found today simmer in his mind. If they were found, he could get back home and put this whole thing behind him. Not to mention, he'd be able to get some real medical attention for Duke.

Liam paused. That's where he should be focusing his attention. On Duke. The one thing in his life that never let him down. Not Madeline or his father. But man's best friend. Having a job to focus on had renewing effects on Liam's mood. He'd channel all his frustration into getting Duke rescued. And once he was better, the two of them would escape the world that seemed to want to crush him.

Rolling his shoulders back, he took a step forward. A crack sounded behind him, followed by a shooting pain in his shoulder. He opened his mouth, but the sound never reached his ears. The force of whatever hit him pushed him forward, and he smacked his head on the tree in front of him. He blinked a few times before he slipped into the fuzzy darkness that surrounded him.

Madeline

The whirring sound of the helicopter blades matched her beating heart. Liam was stretched out on the grass as Bill, the idiot who shot him, paced next to them.

"I really thought he was an animal," Bill kept saying. Like an annoying message on repeat.

Madeline glanced over to study Liam. His eyes were closed, and his skin was pale. She shifted against the hard ground. She'd almost had a heart attack when Bill emerged from the woods, dragging Liam's limp body behind him.

Her stomach twisted as she kept her fingers pressed into his shoulder. The bleeding had slowed, which was a good sign. But he needed medical help as soon as possible.

The trees bent as the helicopter landed next to them. Its roar deafened her to Bill's chant. She swallowed as she reached out and grasped Liam's hand. Feelings of guilt and worry raced through her.

From the corner of her eye, she saw two men jump from the helicopter. They grabbed a stretcher and rolled it over to them. Bill had had a satellite phone and, apparently, Alice had been quite vigilant in searching for Liam. There had been a search team fifty miles out.

"We've got this, ma'am," one of the medics said, waving at her to move away.

"Oh, okay," she muttered, shock still racing through her veins.

Not sure what to do, she stood there, helpless. They took his vitals and then heaved him up onto the stretcher.

"Let's go," the other medic said, cupping her elbow with his gloved hand.

She nodded and began to walk toward the helicopter. Duke. She'd forgotten about Duke. She paused. "The dog," she said, nodding over to his body.

The medic looked in the direction she motioned. "I'll get him. You get on the helicopter," he yelled.

She turned and climbed in after Liam. When the medic boarded with Duke in his arms, the pilot took off.

Madeline wrapped her arms around her stomach. Every feeling, from relief to frustration, to worry, coursed through her veins. They were rescued. In a matter of moments, she would be back to civilization with this whole thing behind her.

But, as she glanced down at Duke and Liam, a tear escaped and raced down her cheek. She'd give that all up if it meant that these two could be okay. She'd gladly take their place if it meant they wouldn't be hurt.

As she swallowed against the lump in her throat, she glanced out the window. The truth was, she was in love. And that thought scared her more than anything she'd faced through the entire Alaskan wilderness.

CHAPTER EIGHTEEN

MADELINE
Two Days Later

*M*adeline sat on her faded red chair, staring out the window. It was drizzling in Seattle, which was nothing new. The raindrops clung to the glass and then slipped down, leaving a trail as it went. She shivered and pulled her blanket around her. Even though she'd been back for two days now, she couldn't get the constant chill out of her bones. It must have been from the trauma. That was it.

"You okay?" Bridget asked, walking up from behind her. She held a steaming mug in her hands.

Madeline tucked her feet farther under her as she nodded. "I think so."

Bridget handed her the mug then sat on an equally faded blue floral chair. She clicked her tongue as she stared at Madeline. It made Madeline feel uncomfortable, so she shifted.

"What?" she asked. But she already knew what her roommate was thinking. Bridget had attempted to get her to talk about the ordeal since she got back, but Madeline couldn't bring herself to form the words.

"Madame Tremone said that you need to start talking. Whatever happened to you is affecting your aura. It's like . . . black," Bridget said, shaking her head as her gaze ran up and down Madeline's body.

Madeline groaned and tilted her head back. She didn't want Bridget talking to her psychic about her, and she certainly didn't want to talk about Liam and what had happened in Alaska. She preferred to just move forward and forget everything she'd gone though.

"I just . . . can't," Madeline whispered.

Bridget sat back. "Okay. When can you?"

Madeline shrugged as she brought the tea up to her lips. She winced as the scalding hot liquid coated her throat. "I don't know."

Bridget opened her lips to say something, but before any words came out, Madeline's phone rang.

Reaching out, Madeline picked it up and groaned. It was Parker. He'd thankfully given her a few days off, seeing how she'd just gone through a life-threatening ordeal, but he ended the call with the understanding that he still expected her to write the article, no matter what had happened.

She chewed her lip as she peeked over at Bridget.

"He's not going to leave you alone," Bridget said, waving to her phone.

Still. Madeline didn't want to talk to her editor right now. All she wanted to do was crawl under her blanket and disappear. Live in a world where she didn't hurt people and they didn't hurt her. So, she shoved the phone under her leg and listened to its muffled rings until it died out.

Whew. That was over. Hopefully, Parker would get the message and just leave her alone.

Bridget's phone began to ring. She pulled it from her back

pocket, glanced at the screen, and then up to Madeline.

"Is Parker calling you?"

Bridget nodded as she swiped her finger across the screen.

"Don't—"

But Bridget already had the phone up to her cheek. "Hello?"

Madeline could hear Parker's muffled voice from where she sat. Bridget kept her gaze fixed on her as she nodded.

"Oh, I agree. She needs to get out of this funk."

Madeline narrowed her eyes. Why was her best friend betraying her like this?

"Yep. The story needs to come out so they can both move forward."

They. Madeline tucked her blanket around her shoulders as Liam's face flashed in her mind. The memories were too painful to relive, so she forced them down with all the strength she could muster.

"Okay. I'll tell her." Bridget pulled the phone from her ear and tapped the side of it. The screen went black. She tucked it back into her pocket and turned to Madeline. "Get up," she said, standing and motioning for Madeline to do the same.

Madeline buried her face into the blanket. "No."

Bridget tugged on the blanket, and it slipped from Madeline's fingers and floated to the floor.

"I am not going to let you go all Brett-breakup on me now. You are going to stand up. You are going to take a shower. And you are going to do your job. You are a strong woman. That story needs to get written so Parker will leave you and, more importantly, me alone." Bridget stared down at her. Her gaze unrelenting.

"But—"

"No. Now." She jutted her finger toward the bathroom.

Madeline widened her eyes as she stared at her crazed roommate. She racked her brain for an excuse, but nothing came. Closing her eyes, she took a deep breath. Fine. She'd do what

Bridget said, but when she was finished, she was going to find another place to live.

She stood and walked into the bathroom. She shut the door and turned the water on. Steam filled the bathroom as she stepped into the shower. The water hit her back as she turned to stare at the wall.

The memory of Liam getting dragged from the woods by that hunter flashed through her mind. The ringing in her ears was as clear today as the moment she realized he'd been shot. But nothing compared to the pain she felt when she was walking behind the gurney as they rushed him into Anchorage General, and he told her to go home. That they were rescued, and he was done with her.

A sob escaped her lips as she buried her face under the water. Her heart broke as the words she wished she'd said raced through her mind. There hadn't been any time to fix what she'd broken. She couldn't go back and change what she'd said. What she'd written.

She washed her hair with a bit more force than normal. When she was clean, she wrapped a towel around her head and one around her body and stepped out. She stared into the mirror. The gash she'd gotten from the plane crash was nearly healed. She reached up and touched the scar that was forming. The memory of Liam's fingers as they brushed her skin caused her to shiver.

Why did he have to hate her like he did? Why had she been such an idiot? It was as if she was always out to sabotage herself.

"You almost done?" Bridget called from the other side of the door. She pounded a few times on it as if to emphasize her words.

Of course. Slave driver Bridget wasn't going to let Madeline take any time to self-loathe. Madeline walked over to the door and unlocked it.

"Good. I was worried you'd been washed down the drain." She grabbed onto Madeline's hand and pulled her into her bedroom. "Now, I've laid out some clothes for you." She nodded to the bed.

Madeline groaned. A pair of jeans and a T-shirt lay across her comforter. "What is this?"

"Just because you won't tell me what happened in Alaska doesn't mean you should lose your job. Parker needs that Davenport article finished by tonight, and it's time to write about it." Her bright blue eyes sparkled as she smiled at Madeline.

Madeline wanted to say no. She wanted to become a hermit in her house. That entire article forced her to relive every minute, good or bad, of being stranded in the wilderness. Every minute she'd spent with Liam. She wasn't sure her heart could take the pain. Avoidance had become the best policy for her. "Bri, I don't know."

Bridget shook her head. "Just get dressed. That's all I'm asking."

Madeline eyed the clothes. Fine. She'd do it. But there was no guarantee that she would write that article. Hopefully, her manic roommate would forget about what she was doing and Madeline would be able to slip back into her PJs and escape from the world. Escape from responsibility. Escape from Liam.

LIAM

The silk sheets underneath Liam were soft. Almost too soft. The beeping next to him filled the silence as he shifted on top of his mattress. A searing pain shot through his shoulder, and he cursed. He needed to stop moving, but being back in his room was strange. It had only been five days since he was shot, and he was already itching to leave.

A knock drew his attention toward the door.

"Come in," he called. Hopefully, it was his doctor and he was here to say everything was fine and that Liam could finally return to his day-to-day activities.

When Alice appeared in the doorway, he groaned. Great. That was not who he wanted to see. She'd been all business since the hospital discharged him into the care of the doctor who Alice had hired. Apparently, she wanted full access to him, and trips to and from the hospital was just too much.

"Glad to see you're up," she said, as she peered at him from above her glasses.

He shrugged. What he really wanted to do was run away. Pack up and leave this place. Every time he closed his eyes, the image of Madeline's crushed expression haunted him. But he didn't want her hanging around him just because he'd been shot. And besides, didn't she tell him that he should always be honest?

He swallowed. The same hollow feeling took up residence in his gut as a familiar thought slammed into the back of his mind. The one that told him, he hadn't been honest at all. To himself or to Madeline.

Liam cleared his throat. He didn't want to think about that right now. She'd moved on and so had he. Or at least, he was going to. As soon as he was no longer attached to these monitors.

Alice walked over and pulled open the drapes. "Did you see the article?" she asked, turning to look at him.

"Article? What article?" Why was Alice being so cryptic?

She walked over to her purse, pulled out a copy of *The Journal,* and handed it over to him. "It was published a few days ago. Flip to page thirty-five. I'm sure you'll find it enlightening."

Liam studied her as he reached over and grabbed the magazine. He glanced at the cover. "Stranded with the Billionaire" was printed in large letters at the bottom of the page. His stomach churned. So she'd written it. The terrible article that she called journalistic brilliance was now available for the entire world to see.

He pushed it to the edge of the bed. "Not interested."

Alice glanced at him. "Really?"

"I'm not interested in reading crap."

Her eyebrows knitted together. "Crap?"

"Trust me, I saw the beginning of that article while in Alaska. I'm not interested in reading the final version."

"But—"

"Are you here for anything else?" he asked. He was ready to move this conversation forward.

Alice pushed her glassed up her nose and nodded. "We have some things to take care of this morning." She nodded at Liam. "You'll need to get dressed for this. You can come in," she called toward the door.

Two nurses and a maid carrying a suit walked in. They made their way over to him and pulled the sheets back. Startled, Liam winced, which caused his shoulder to throb.

"What's happening?" he asked as he grabbed at the covers.

Alice's eyes widened. "Liam, I understand you've been through a horrendous ordeal. But"—she raised her finger—"you have a responsibility to the company. No more lounging in bed."

"But I thought I'd gained a lot of sympathy with the plane crash." He winced. He hated that Alice had used the place crash for publicity.

"Yes. But the news is only satisfied for so long. We're are going to hold a press conference here, where you will share the information we'd planned for you to share in Denali." Her phone rang as she headed toward the open door. She paused and leaned over to one of the nurses. "Make sure his sling is obvious," she said and then slipped out.

Liam cringed but kept his lips shut. He allowed the nurses to help him from the bed and into the shower. Once he was dressed with his sling showcased in front of him, Alice returned.

She smiled as she walked across the room. Liam chewed his cheek. He hated that Alice was making him do this. He hated this life.

"What now?" She sighed as she neared him. Her gaze ran up and down him and she nodded in the other women's direction. They whispered to each other as they left the room.

"I guess I'm just not ready," Liam said. His voice gruffer than he intended.

Alice stopped and stared at him. "You have to stop doing that," she said as she reached out and wiped at one of his shoulders.

Heat raced up his back. What did she know? "Doing what?"

"Running away," she said. Alice always had a way of saying things straight. She never pulled any punches. The truth was more valuable to her than anything else.

"I don't run away."

She stared at him. "Liam Richard Davenport, I have known you your whole life." She paused as she folded her arms. "I've seen the good, the bad, and the ugly sides of you."

He scoffed but didn't deny it. It was true.

"You run away when you're scared." She stepped back and adjusted her glasses.

Liam let his lips fall open. He wanted to say that she was wrong. He wanted to justify all of his past behavior. But he couldn't form the words to say anything. The more he thought about it, the truer the statement became.

"Why are you scared this time? What happened to you in Alaska that you're not telling me? I already know Madeline's side of everything." She nodded to the magazine on his bed.

Liam wanted to die under her scrutiny. If he even tried to lie, would she know? It seemed like she had a sixth sense about these things.

"Tell me."

"But I didn't admit to it."

Alice smiled. "You didn't have to. Your silence tells me everything." She settled in on the armchair next to the window. "Out with it."

Liam sighed and leaned against the wall. It was hard to find the words to explain what happened. Especially when he wasn't sure what had happened. But he laid it all out in front of Alice. He held nothing back. He told her about the trip down the mountain.

About how Madeline almost died in the glacier lake. How they fought yet still had moments where he felt like he could tell her anything. About the kiss.

Alice's eyes widened as he talked about how Duke got injured to save Madeline. He told her about the article and then how he got shot. And then he ended it with how he told Madeline to leave him alone.

The air grew silent as Liam's final words hung there. He glanced over to Alice who had her elbows propped up on the armrests and her fingers pressed together in front of her. He watched her, waiting for a response.

"Do you understand now why I needed to leave her?" Why did he so desperately want Alice to approve of the way he'd dismissed Madeline? He was supposed to be a confident man. Just like his father. Yet, for some reason, his words felt like acid in his throat.

"That's what you think was the best thing?" Alice's voice was quiet as she eyed him.

"Yes?"

She stared at him. "If that's what you think is best, then there's nothing that I can say that will change your mind."

Great. What did that mean? Why was Alice being so cryptic? "You don't think what I did was the right thing?"

Alice's eyes narrowed. "Liam, you're a great guy. But you don't know how to love someone completely."

"Wait, who said anything about love?"

She gave him a pointed look. "You can't lie to me, Liam. You're scared to love Madeline. Without reserve. No matter what. Loving her and letting her in."

His stomach churned. Why did her words leave him feeling so uneasy? Could he expose himself like that? He knew the tension and attraction was there between him and Madeline. But the trust has been broken. And he wasn't sure they could come back from that.

"But do you think she could forgive me? Love me back?"

Alice sighed as she stood. "I think you should read that article."

Liam's gaze fell to the shiny pages of *The Journal*. Alice seemed convinced that whatever Madeline had written was going to change his mind.

"You're going to do what you want to do, Liam. When you want to know what you should do, then come ask me." She waved to the door. "We have damage control. Let's do it."

Liam slipped on his shoes and moved to follow after her. He stopped when he reached his bed. He leaned over and grabbed the magazine. He might get bored in the car. That was all. It wasn't because he was now curious about what Madeline had said about him. What she thought about their time together.

He shut his door and made his way down the hall. He'd worry about his feelings for Madeline after this PR nightmare was over. Right now, it was taking all of his brainpower to focus on cleaning up his dad's messes, much less his own.

CHAPTER NINETEEN

MADELINE

The familiar thrill that would race over Madeline as she stood next to fellow journalist and photographers during a press conference wasn't having the same effect on her this time. Still reeling over the fact that she hadn't dissuaded Bridget from forcing her to go, she folded her arms across her chest. Her skirt was riding up, and her heels were squeezing her feet. It didn't help that the blisters weren't fully healed from the ski boots Liam had made her wear five days ago.

Plus, Bridget had decided that a press conference sounded extremely interesting and chose to stay and stand right next to Madeline. That made the chance of a hasty exit nearly impossible.

Bridget tapped Madeline's arm as she grinned over at her. "You never told me how fun these things were," she said as her eyes danced with amusement.

Madeline stared at her. "Probably because they're not," she said. What was exciting were her bed and her covers. A place where she could hide and the rest of the world didn't know her. A place where Liam Davenport didn't exist.

Agh, why couldn't she just stop thinking about him? Why wouldn't he just leave her alone? He had all but told her he wasn't interested. Why wasn't her heart getting the memo?

Her article had been out for two days now, and she'd heard nothing from Liam. Her cheeks burned as she thought about the truths she'd told in it. She'd exposed herself and her feelings in a way that she'd never done before.

His silence was like a slap in the face. The worst kind of rejection. Even though Parker said it was the best article she'd ever written, the only praise she longed for was Liam's, and she'd given up hope that he'd ever give it to her.

She sighed and looked around. Why were all these people gathered here anyways? Bridget had been very cryptic about why they were coming here. She glanced around at fellow journalists who were chatting with one another. The word "survivor" caught her attention causing her to lean in.

"I know, right? I can't believe they're having this press conference days after he was found," one reporter said as she fiddled with the recorder in her hand.

Found? What did that mean? She glanced over at Bridget who staring at a particularly good-looking photographer that was switching out his camera lens. Oh, no.

"Bridget, why are we here? What is this press conference for?"

Bridget glanced over at her. Her eyes widened as if she had been caught. "Mad, you have to understand you wouldn't have come if I told you who this was for."

Madeline's heart fell out of her body. Her cheeks heated as the room faded around her. She was here to see Liam Davenport give a press conference. She wanted to cry and throw up at the same time. What had Bri done? She needed to leave. Now.

Just as she turned to make a hasty exit, all the reporters and photographers pushed in around her. There was a commotion on the stage. She kept her back to the podium as she stared at the far exit, wishing somehow she could make it there.

A voice came over the microphone. It was feminine and had a no-nonsense tone that Madeline recognized. Alice.

"I want to thank you all for coming here today. I'm hoping we can make this brief as Mr. Davenport is still recovering from his trauma that he endured this past week. I would like to keep the questions to a minimum so that we can get out of here in a timely matter. With that being said, I am going to turn the time over to Mr. Liam Davenport, CEO of Davenport Outdoors."

Madeline closed her eyes as she heard some shuffling behind her and then the clearing of a throat into the microphone. She braced herself as she waited to hear the smooth voice that had become a constant in her life for those few fateful days.

"As many as you know, my late father, Richard Davenport, had numerous accounts of illegal poaching brought against him."

Her heart pounded at the familiar cadence of his voice. It caused tears to form on her eyelids. Why was she here? Why was Bridget torturing her this way?

"On behalf of everyone at Davenport Outdoors, I want to sincerely apologize to all the loyal customers and supporters this company has had over the years. What my father did was unacceptable and wrong. And I hope, from the bottom of my heart, that people can find it within themselves to forgive us."

Madeline stopped. There was something in the tone of Liam's voice that caused her to turn around. She hesitated and then let her gaze find its way up to the podium. Her heart skipped a beat. Liam was staring straight at her. His dark eyes were piercing and serious.

"We were wrong. So very wrong. And though we don't deserve forgiveness for what we've done, we hope that eventually, through time, the world can forgive the Davenports."

Liam's gaze never left her face. Soon, the journalist and photographers that were standing around her turned to look at her. Madeline's whole body heated at the attention this with causing.

Some harsh whispering drew people's attention back to the podium. Alice was whispering things into Liam's ear. Liam turned to say something to her, and their conversation could be heard over the speakers.

"Why didn't you tell me she would be here?"

Alice turned to the crowd and smiled. Then she leaned back toward Liam. "The donations," she whispered.

Liam stared at her for a second then turn back around to the microphone. "Davenport Outdoors has agreed to donate ten million dollars to the reserves in every country that my father illegally poached in. Although we know this cannot right the wrong, we hope that this can start to heal the pain that was caused by his actions."

He glanced over to Alice, who nodded. As if it were the release he was looking for, he turned and sprinted down the stairs. Alice approached the microphone and nodded in the direction of the audience. Hands flew up, and questions peppered the air.

"Wow. That was exciting," Bridget said as she glanced over to Madeline.

"Why did you do this?" Madeline squeaked as she tried to keep her emotions at bay.

Bridget wrapped her arm around Madeline's shoulders. "Honey, you need to move on. Either with him or without him. You needed to see him. Start the healing process."

Madeline opened her lips to say something, but nothing came out. Instead, she felt as if the building was closing in on her. In desperate need of fresh air, Madeline just nodded and shoved her way through the crowd toward the exit. She ducked her head as she pushed open the metal door and stepped out onto the bustling sidewalk.

She collapsed against the brick building and buried her face in her hands. Was Liam talking about them? Was he apologizing for what he had done? Did he see her article? Did he know how she felt?

Everything about this made her feel sick. There was peace in knowing he hadn't read her article. In knowing that the words she had written, even though she didn't regret writing them, might not have been seen by him. She had said that being stranded in the wilderness with him had been the greatest adventure she had ever taken. That she would never go back and change what happened.

But now that there was a possibility he knew every last detail of her heart that she'd spilled onto the paper, she wasn't sure how to handle it. Now, all she wanted to do was crawl into a hole and disappear. Forever.

"Madeline?" Liam's deep voice asked from behind her.

Her skin tingled as she became very aware of how close he was standing to her. It took all of her strength to pull her hands away from her face and glanced over. Liam was now next to her with his hands shoved in his front pocket and his shoulders slumped. Had he been as miserable without her as she had been without him?

"Yes?" she whispered. She was afraid that if she were too loud, she might scare him away.

His eyebrows furrowed as he reached behind him. He emerged with a magazine that was rolled up. It was *The Journal.* Her article.

She straightened. She wasn't going to let him go this time without telling him exactly what she thought. Liam Davenport was going to listen to her, one way or another. Even if it meant he might reject her, she was going to say her piece. Only then could she truly move on.

LIAM

Liam tried to steady his nerves as he stared down at Madeline. Her tear-stained face and red eyes pulled at his heart in ways he'd never experienced before. All he wanted to do at this moment was pull her into his arms and comfort her.

But, there were a few things that needed to be said before he could do that. And they all had to do with the article.

On the way to the press conference, he'd pulled out the magazine, ready to hate the words Madeline had written. After all, he'd seen the first draft. But the further he got into it, the more he realized that she'd changed everything.

"Did you mean this?" he asked, flipping the magazine open to her article. "Or were you just trying to sell copies?"

Madeline's gaze fell to the page and then made its way back up to him. She studied his gaze for a moment before she nodded. "Yes," she whispered.

His heart pounded so hard that he could hear it in his ears. "Yes, you were trying to sell magazines, or yes, you meant"—he leaned down to study the words as if he hadn't already memorized what she'd written—"'To some, Liam Davenport is a pretentious party boy with no thought to how the rest of the world lives. It's that type of lifestyle that sells stories. But I'm here today to debunk those ridiculous articles. What I've learned from being stranded with party boy Davenport is that there is so much more.'"

She dropped his gaze and kept it trained on the sidewalk beneath their feet. When she didn't say anything, he scanned further down the article to a particularly confusing section.

"How about this part? 'With no thought of his own life, Liam jumped into the water to save mine. Me. A journalist who prided herself on finding out facts but instead allowed her own prejudices to cloud her judgment. On all accounts, he should have left me there. But he couldn't. There is a sense of duty and pride to Mr. Davenport, one that could not coexist with someone who feels as if they were above the law. From my time with Liam in the wilderness, I discovered that there was absolutely no way he could've been involved with the actions of his late father.'"

Liam glanced up to see Madeline staring at him. There was

strength in her gaze that told him she had meant every word. He swallowed as his throat dried.

"And what about this?" he asked, his voice growing raspy from the lack of moisture. "'I think the most important thing I discovered while fighting for my life on the Alaskan wilderness was just how similar Liam Davenport and I were. We were both orphaned by our parents. Desperate to find our place in the world. And seeking for the one thing that everyone looks for: love. The kind that fills your soul and repairs the cracks that life has created. And as much as it scares me to say, I found that. In the depths of the wilderness, I fell in love with the billionaire.'" His voice faded as the last word rolled off his tongue. He paused before raising his gaze to meet hers.

A tear rolled down her cheek, and out of instinct he reached up and wiped it away. His fingers tingled as the sensation of her skin raced up his arm.

"Madeline, is this the truth?" He desperately needed to know the answer.

She chewed her lip and then slowly began to nod. "I meant every word," she whispered.

That was exactly what he wanted to hear. He reached out and wrapped his arm around her waist and pulled her toward him. He reveled in the feeling of her body next to his. The familiarity of her curves against him. Her shoulders shook as small sobs escaped her lips.

"I'm sorry," he said, peering down at her. "I am so very sorry for the way I treated you. You didn't deserve it."

A smile played on her lips as she wiped her tears and glanced up at him. She moved to speak, but he shook his head. He wasn't done.

"You are the single best thing that has ever happened to me. You taught me how to be strong, how to take responsibility, and how to love more deeply than I ever imagined possible." He tightened his grip on her as if he were afraid that she would disappear. "Please, forgive me. Forgive this fool who was completely wrapped up in his pride to admit that he, too, found love in the wilderness."

"Can I speak now?"

Liam nodded.

"I forgive you," she said as she rose up onto her tiptoes and pressed her lips against his.

Heat raced across his body as he pulled her toward him to deepen the kiss. His heart sang as he wrapped his good arm around her. She tangled her fingers into his hair. For a moment, everything faded away. They were no longer journalist and billionaire, but a guy who was desperately in love with a girl. And he never wanted this moment to end.

When she pulled away, he groaned. He never wanted her to leave his presence again.

"How's Duke?" she breathed as she glanced up at him.

"My dog? You stopped that kiss to talk about my dog?"

She giggled and swiped at his shoulder. "Come on."

Liam tightened his grip on her, so she laid her head against his chest.

"He misses you," Liam said.

"He does?"

"Yep."

Madeline giggled. "Good, because I have some news."

Liam pulled back. "What?"

"You're never going to guess."

He narrowed his eyes at her.

"I got a puppy."

"Really? The girl who was terrified of Duke got a dog?"

She nodded. "I guess you're not the only one who had an effect on me."

Liam pulled her back and rested his chin on her head. "I love you," he whispered.

"I love you, too."

In that moment, Liam was happy. In that moment, Liam knew that this was all he was ever going to need. He'd found his person and, in her, his home.

EPILOGUE

16 months later

Snow fell outside the window as Liam paced in front of it. He glanced down at his watch. Madeline was an hour late. Where was she?

A Christmas ballad played softly in the background. Alice had done an amazing job finding a decorator to deck out this cabin. A Christmas tree sat in the far corner with twinkling lights. Duke lay next to it with Madeline's present tied to his collar.

Everything was perfect. Except for the fact that Madeline was not here. He sighed and ran his hands through his hair. His suit felt as if it were strangling him. He wasn't sure if it was his nerves because he was about to ask Madeline to marry him. Or from the fact that he worried Alaska may have claimed her once more.

He should have known better than to reserve a cabin in the mountains of Alaska. But, for some reason, he thought it would be romantic to go back to the place where they fell in love Man, he could be stupid sometimes.

He should have taken Alice's parted lips and raised eyebrows as a sign when he told her what he had planned. But it seemed like the perfect proposal.

Headlights flashed by the window, and Liam's heart picked up speed. She was here. Finally.

Grabbing his coat, he raced outside. Daniel, his driver, was opening the back door. He glanced over at Liam.

"Everything okay?" Liam asked.

Daniel looked a bit pale. "Not quite used to these winding roads."

Liam reached out and patted his shoulder. "Sorry, man."

Daniel shrugged. "Well, we got here, didn't we?"

Peering into the limo, Liam looked for Madeline. She was wrapped up under a blanket with her head tucked out of sight.

"Madeline?" he asked, slipping onto the seat next to her.

She emerged with her eyes wide. "What. The. Heck," she whispered as her gaze darted around the limo.

Liam reached out and pulled her toward him. "I'm so sorry. I don't why I thought this would be romantic. I'm such an idiot." He leaned down and kissed her on the head.

Madeline's ridged posture seemed to relax as she leaned into him. "Not one of your smartest ideas."

Liam's heart sank. This proposal was not going as planned. How could he have been such an idiot?

"Come on. Let's go inside and get some hot cocoa."

Madeline nodded into his shoulder. "Okay."

In under five minutes, her luggage was unloaded and in the house. Madeline was cuddled on the couch as Liam walked Daniel to the limo.

"Thanks, man," he said, patting Daniel on the shoulder. "I owe you a big Christmas bonus."

Daniel's eyes brightened. "Yeah, okay," he said, giving Liam a smile.

"Just tell Alice I approved whatever you think." It was Christmas. Whatever he could do to keep his employees happy, he'd do it.

"Good luck," Daniel said as he nodded toward the cabin. "She really has no idea."

Nerves raced through Liam's stomach at the mention of his plan. "Yeah, I hope I didn't blow it with the whole Alaska bit."

Daniel shrugged. "I'm sure she'll get over it."

Liam nodded as Daniel shut the door and pulled down the driveway. Taking a deep breath, Liam walked back inside.

Duke had left his corner and was happily sitting next to Madeline. She'd finally emerged from the covers and was petting his head. She looked calmer, more put-together.

"Daniel gone?" she asked.

Liam nodded. His stomach was knotted as he watched her hand get dangerously close to the engagement ring he'd secured to Duke's collar.

"Hey, Duke." He whistled. Duke just gave him an unimpressed look and turned back to Madeline.

She laughed. "Still love me over Liam, huh?" she asked, grabbing both sides of Duke's face and bringing it closer to her. "I'm so mad that Bridget got Jersey for the holiday. She would have loved seeing you."

"He'll bite you," Liam blurted out. He could see the ring flash between the folds of fur. This had to be the worst proposal in the history of proposals. Terrifying the girl and then her discovering the ring before even getting a chance to ask.

Madeline glanced over to him. "What is wrong with you? Duke doesn't bite." She leaned in and let Duke lick her cheek.

"He just threw up!" Liam shouted this time. Anything to get her away from his dog.

"Liam Davenport, why would you say that?" she asked as she reached out and wiped her face with her sleeve. "And why are you acting so strange? You're the one who asked me up here." She pushed farther from Duke but kept her hand resting on his head. He'd relaxed next to her, resting his body next to her.

"I—" His heart hammered in his chest. Should he just do it? Stop this ridiculous planning and just ask?

"What's this?"

Too late. She was fingering the ring tied to Duke's neck.

Dropping down to one knee, Liam grabbed Madeline's other hand and peered up at her.

"Liam," she breathed as her gaze fell to their hands.

"Madeline Abernathy. I love you more than I've ever loved anyone or anything."

Duke barked.

"Even more than I love Duke." He swallowed as he met her gaze head-on. "You are the single best thing to ever happen to me. You are the only person I want say goodnight to and the only person I want to see when I wake up in the morning. You are my soul mate. My person. Would you do the honor of becoming my wife?" The words spilled from his lips at record speed. The cadence of his voice matched the pounding of his heart.

She studied him.

He swallowed. Why wasn't she saying anything?

"Liam Davenport, I thought you'd never ask." She slipped off the couch and knelt in front of him. She grabbed his other hand with hers and peered up at him. "I'll marry you on one condition."

Liam nodded. "Anything."

"We never come to Alaska again."

Liam laughed as he pulled her toward him and pressed his lips to hers. He leaned back and glanced down at her. "I can make that deal, my love," he said, and then leaned in for another kiss.

Stay tuned for the next book

FALLING FOR THE BILLIONAIRE

She's a baker trying to make it in NYC. He's a billionaire with a golden touch. When a friendly philanthropy search creates feelings neither were expecting, they need to decide if love is worth trusting.

Take me to Amazon

TRY ANNE-MARIE'S NEW LINE OF CONTEMPORARY YA ROMANCES

RULE #1: YOU CAN'T DATE THE COACH'S DAUGHTER

Book 1 of the Rules of Love Series

Release Date July 2018

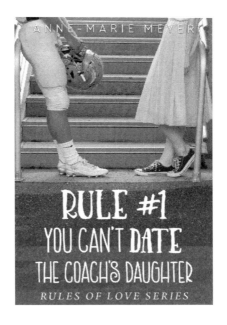

Grab it from Amazon HERE

OTHER BOOKS BY ANNE-MARIE MEYER

CLEAN ADULT ROMANCES

Forgetting the Billionaire

Book 1 of the Clean Billionaire Romance series

Forgiving the Billionaire

Book 2 of the Clean Billionaire Romance series

Finding Love with the Billionaire

Book 3 of the Clean Billionaire Romance series

Falling for the Billionaire

Book 4 of the Clean Billionaire Romance series

Fixing the Billionaire

Book 5 of the Clean Billionaire Romance series

The Complete Billionaire Series

The Whole Series for $9.99

Marrying a Cowboy

Book 1 of a Fake Marriage series

Fighting Love for the Cowboy

Book 1 of A Moose Falls Romance

Marrying an Athlete

Book 2 of a Fake Marriage series

Marrying a Billionaire

Book 3 of a Fake Marriage series

Marrying a Prince

Book 4 of a Fake Marriage series

CLEAN YA ROMANCES

Rule #1: You Can't Date the Coach's Daughter

Book 1 of the Rules of Love series

GRAB A FREE NOVELLA BY ANNE-MARIE MEYER

It's not to late! Sign up for Anne-Marie Meyer's newsletter and grab your free copy of

Love Under Contract

A Swan Princess inspired novella

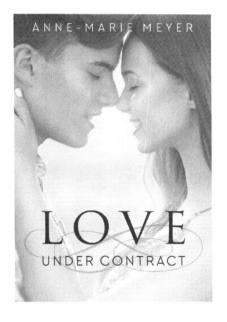

TAKE ME TO MY FREE NOVELLA

GRAB ALL 5 SWEET BILLIONAIRE ROMANCES FOR $9.99

If you love swoon worthy, clean romance, grab all 5 Sweet Billionaire Romances for only $9.99! Free in KU.

That's a $5.00 savings!

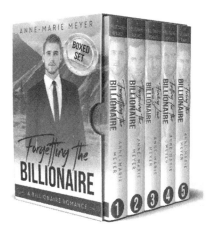

Head over to Amazon HERE

ABOUT THE AUTHOR

Anne-Marie Meyer lives in MN with her husband, four boys, and baby girl. She loves romantic movies and believes that there is a FRIENDS quote for just about every aspect of life.

Connect with Anne-Marie on these platforms!
anne-mariemeyer.com

f